the OPIUM SMUGGLER

CELINE JEANJEAN

The Opium Smuggler

http://celinejeanjean.com

ISBN-13: 9782492523144

Requests to publish work from this book should be sent to:
Celine@celinejeanjean.com

Cover by bonobobookcovers.com
Story and stylistic edit by redadeptediting.com
Copy Edit and Proofread by Kath Macfarlane
(kathy.macfarlane2011@gmail.com)

Prologue

Jeremiah sat on the step before his front door, watching as his daughter, Adelma, considered taking her first step. It was late afternoon, the sun low and yellow. It made a fine halo of Adelma's dark baby curls, tingeing them with gold, and turned the sea in the Damsian Enclosed Docks to the colour of beaten brass.

The mad chaos of the docks was starting to slow, leaving ships to sway gently in their berths, their masts like a forest jutting out of the sea. A few voices still rang out here and there, final orders being called as dockworkers wrapped everything up for the evening.

Jeremiah's house opened directly onto the docks, the perfect spot for a fisherman. He had lived in that house his whole life and had grown up among the smells of the docks. Back when Damsport was just a slum, the smells of rotten seafood had mixed with the thick waft of silt and algae, but now it was a whole other kettle of fish. Old spices, animal dung, meat on the turn that glistened with an oily sheen, sweat from all the dock workers, bruised fruit, spoiled vegetables, and lots he couldn't identify mingled together as more and more ships arrived each day, bringing exotic cargo.

There was a new smell, too, of late—the acrid coal smoke of steam-powered boats. They were an unusual sight, so the one carefully manoeuvring out in the docks was drawing a crowd. Its engine coughed and wheezed heavy puffs of black smoke from its single chimney as it moved awkwardly.

"Steam power," Jeremiah scoffed to himself. He turned to Adelma. "Ridiculous. That'll never take, my girl. You mark my words. Ain't replacing a good sail and a strong wind. Them fools what are working with steam are wasting their time. Now come on, come to your Da." He stretched out his arms.

Adelma gurgled happily, stretching her own arms open in reply and swaying like a drunken sailor on her chubby legs, but still, she didn't walk.

"One foot in front of the other now," Jeremiah coaxed, still gesturing with his hands.

Adelma squealed and gurgled again. Then she seemed to decide to move forward and lost her balance, falling back on her bum. She hiccupped from the shock of it, looking up at her father, her mouth an *O* of surprise. She wore only a yellowed cloth nappy, the fabric speaking of the many, many washes it had been through. Her bare brown belly bulged over the top of it. She was so small, so fragile, her brown skin looking pale compared to Jeremiah's weather-beaten and sun-darkened hide.

Jeremiah laughed, and Adelma broke into a smile in response, delighted. "Come on, my girl." Jeremiah set her back on her feet. "Let's try again."

Today was Adelma's first birthday, and so Jeremiah had taken the day off from fishing to mourn and celebrate. Adelma's mother—also called Adelma, as Jeremiah had named his daughter for his wife—had died in childbirth.

"Come on, Adelma," Jeremiah repeated, waggling his fingers.

She took a hesitant step, wobbling dangerously.

"There you go… There you go!" Jeremiah called out excitedly, prouder than a peacock on parade day. "There you go, my darling girl. Come to your Da."

A couple walked past at that moment. Their clothes were expensive enough to make it clear they weren't from this part of town. The woman held on to the crook of her husband's arm, her nose wrinkling in disgust at the riot of smells. She cast a glance at Jeremiah and Adelma.

Adelma chose that moment to take her second wobbly step, falling forward. Jeremiah caught her and swept her up in his arms, laughing. "I gotcha. You remember that, my girl. Your old man's always got your back."

He felt a twinge of sadness at the words. Adelma should have had a mother standing behind her, too. Jeremiah felt oh-so keenly aware of his responsibility. He was the *only* person Adelma had in the world. He had to not only keep her safe, but also make sure she would continue to be safe even once his time had come.

"Did you see that girl?" the woman asked her husband as they walked past. "She must be two or maybe three, and she doesn't even walk yet. Disgraceful. I tell you, people in this part of town are little more than savages, and that baby is clearly retarded."

Jeremiah felt a rush of icy anger at the words. Adelma was easily larger than a two-year-old, but no matter how big she was, it didn't make up for the fact that she had only been alive for a year, and therefore couldn't quite walk yet.

He stood up, shifting Adelma so he held her with one arm, keeping her balanced on his hip. He hurried after the couple. "Excuse me."

The couple stopped and looked back, surprised. The woman had the good grace to look sheepish when she caught sight of Adelma.

Jeremiah backhanded the woman across the face hard enough to send her sprawling to the ground in a cry of pain and shock. Before her husband could react, Jeremiah punched him in square in the stomach. The man made a sound like a bladder deflating, and he slowly sank to his knees, groaning with pain.

"My daughter is one year old," he informed the prone woman, who looked up at him with fear, holding her reddening cheek. "She might be big, but she's only one, so it's perfectly normal for her to only be taking her first steps today. In fact, I reckon them was the best first steps anyone's took in the Rookery. So you say anything about my daughter being retarded again, and I'll knock every one of your teeth out. Every. Last. Tooth. Got it?"

Jeremiah turned to the husband. "Nothing personal," he added. "Didn't want to risk you trying to defend your wife. Got my daughter here to think of." He patted Adelma's back. "Couldn't have you swinging for me and hitting my Adelma. It's her birthday, after all."

The husband didn't reply, still curled around his winded stomach.

"It'll take you a while to get your breath back," Jeremiah told him, not unkindly. "I punch pretty damn hard." He turned and walked away.

Adelma had watched the whole scene unfold in silence, her eyes wide. She held on to her father's neck with her chubby arms, looking back over his shoulder. She had her mother's eyes, wide and dark, but everything else about her features came straight from Jeremiah. And he had one ugly mug—a forehead like a stack of books and a nose like a butcher's cleaver. Jeremiah wasn't one for vanity, and he hoped Adelma wouldn't be, either.

He kissed her cheek to reassure her. "You see, Adelma, my girl, that is how we deal with people what insult us. Retaliation is key—never *ever* let a slight against you pass without answering it. I'll teach you how. Don't you worry yourself none for now, my darling girl. Your old Da's gonna keep you safe."

Jeremiah opened his front door and ducked low to pass beneath the doorframe, which had been built for regular-sized people. He knew from experience that the world wasn't always kind to those who were as freakishly big and ugly as him. The jokes, the sniggers, the snide comments saying that only a blind woman would look twice at him. It was likely to be even worse for a girl who looked like that.

Well, he'd make sure Adelma was ready. The world wasn't going to dare say a bad word about her—he'd see to that.

"I got us a special treat for dinner on account that it's your birthday," Jeremiah told Adelma. He blew a raspberry in Adelma's neck, making her squeal with laughter, and then put her down gently. She didn't stay standing for long, dropping down to a sturdier sitting position, keeping her eyes on him. Jeremiah smiled at her and closed the door, shutting out the world and all its nastiness.

Adelma dropped anchor in the quiet little cove she and Kieran had used before. It was the middle of the night, but although there was a full moon, the creek was hidden within thick shadows, keeping them out of sight of anyone watching from the shore.

The tide had begun to go out, revealing a slimy fringe of algae that ringed the base of the rocks, like the last few hairs clinging to a balding man's head. The coast in this part was a jumble of rocks and boulders, giving way a little farther on to a coarse gravel beach. With the low tide, the sea-worn, smooth rocks were going to be so slippery, they might as well be covered with oil. Adelma and Kieran would need to be careful.

Once the ship was secured, Adelma paused, listening to the night. The air was thick with the salty smell of the algae, the waves lapping gently against the rocks. As far as she could tell, all was well. She grinned into the darkness and whispered, "You ready?"

Kieran grunted. That was as much of an answer as she was going to get from him. She figured if there was a problem, he'd make the effort to actually use words. Adelma climbed over the side of the boat, easing herself down into the tiny dinghy that she kept tethered to the side of her ship.

Kieran leaned over to pass her a bundle which she cradled carefully in her hands. That bundle was as dangerous as anything an alchemist could cook up: a rover sea fly nest.

Rover sea flies were no joke, and Adelma had been stung enough times growing up to have a healthy respect for them. They were big, about the size of hornets, and they made their nests in mangroves, building the drop-shaped structures around low branches or roots.

Adelma had no idea why they were called flies—they should have been called something like painful-arse hornets. Rover sea flies made them sound nice and harmless. Probably some stupid scientist wanted to have them named after him.

She'd waited until the flies of this particular nest were all inside and asleep for the night. Then she'd cut off the branch supporting the nest and wrapped it in a cotton cloth. So long as she was careful not to disturb the rovers, she'd be able to carry the nest without trouble.

Kieran slipped down into the dinghy, making it rock. It was so small that when they were both sat in it facing each other, their knees were touching. He had a pack on his back which contained the opium, and Adelma passed him the rover nest. He kept it at arms' length, twisting to the right so it wasn't in Adelma's face. Although it was too dark to see his expression, Adelma knew there'd be quite a lot of fear there. Kieran wasn't the bravest sort.

She untethered the dingy and rowed them to shore. They did some more awkward passing of the nest to and fro as they both clambered off the dinghy and onto the rocks. The rocks felt slick as wet glass beneath Adelma's hands.

Once she had secured the dinghy, they both set off, Adelma carrying the nest once more.

Clambering over the rocks was slow, careful work. They couldn't afford to rush, not when a fall into the sea meant the risk of someone hearing the splash, the opium getting wet, or worse, the nest breaking, releasing the rover flies all over them. An attack by an angry swarm was devastatingly painful, and Adelma needed the nest intact for later.

Once out of the little cove's shadows, Adelma caught sight of the moon shining brightly and illuminating the bay. It cast gleaming reflections over the sea. The song of the waves was now a loud shivering sound as the water withdrew between the thick gravel of the beach.

From the beach, the land rose up steeply, but at this end of the bay it was more a steep climb than an actual cliff. Adelma clambered down from the slippery boulders, her boots sinking an inch into the wet, gravelly sand. She crouched and Kieran joined her.

"You remember the plan? Same as last time. Once I've got them all occupied and focused on me, you slip through and make the delivery."

He nodded, frowning. "I know what I'm doing. Stop fussing."

He was an odd-looking man, although Adelma wasn't really in a position to criticise anybody's appearance. He wasn't as ugly as she was, but there was something of the pigeon about him. He was tall and lanky, with a beak-like nose, bulging eyes, and a prominent Adam's apple. The pigeon impression came when he walked, his head bobbing in rhythm with his steps.

He was also the only person Adelma had found willing to partner up with her in this venture. He could flap his arms like wings and coo or cluck if the fancy took him—she didn't care so long as he did his part of the job.

Adelma stood up and crept towards the steep hill. She found herself grinning. A night spent smuggling was a night well spent. Very well spent. She loved smuggling work and had done ever since she put together her first job. But it was particularly pleasant to be pulling one over on Airnian customs officers.

This part of the Airnian coastline wasn't far from Damsport, but it was far enough from any large town that it was only lightly monitored. Perfect, in short, for a smuggling run.

She made her way up the steep rise slowly, careful to stick to the grass rather than step on the path, where the crunch of gravel might give her away. Jutting rocks at the top of the rise created a natural bottleneck.

Adelma knew customs officers patrolled this area—clearly, she wasn't the only one who'd found it a good smuggling spot in the past. She expected the officers would be sitting on the other side of the bottleneck, playing cards or something of the sort, from the way she could hear them talking softly.

Last time, there had only been a couple—child's play for her to spring on them and knock them out. There was no way to climb over the sheer rocks on either side of the bottleneck or up the cliff face farther up and down the coast.

Adelma planned to repeat the same plan as last time, but she expected to find more people tonight. That was why she'd brought reinforcements in the form of the nest. Moving oh-so-slowly, she carefully unwrapped it.

Then she took a deep breath and threw it up through the bottleneck. She hurriedly ran back a few paces, hearing the nest smash to the ground, followed by the shouts of surprise from the officers.

Immediately, the familiar angry buzzing took up as the flies rushed out of their ruined nest to defend against their perceived attackers.

Adelma and Kieran were prepared with heavy leathers that should protect them against most of the stings. They both pulled scarves around their faces. Adelma waited for the shouts of pain and panic to really have taken hold.

"Alright, here goes." She drew her battle-axes, took a deep breath, and charged forward.

She burst through the bottleneck to find no fewer than ten men and women. A good thing she'd brought the nest. They might not be fighters of her calibre or strength, but ten opponents was still a lot to take on alone.

"She's back," one shouted, and Adelma felt a brief flash of smugness. They remembered her.

She attacked, fast and ruthless. She'd use the flat of her axes rather than the blade, so as to knock out and not kill. If she killed them all, that would attract a lot of unwanted attention from the nearby city. She charged the guard nearest to her, bending at the waist so her shoulder crunched into his ribs. That sent him staggering back.

She spun around, extending both arms. Her battle-axes were still angled to stun, not kill, but the three who'd rushed to attack dodged in time, and she only caught one in the side. Still, the blow was enough to send the woman staggering, wheezing from a winded stomach and cracked ribs.

With a joyful cry, Adelma launched herself at her opponents. They were distracted by the pain of the rover flies. Poor bastards probably hadn't felt the sting of rovers before, whereas Adelma was used to it. Their fighting was poor, at best.

A kick snatched the legs out from under a man, sending him sprawling heavily to the ground. She dropped one axe and punched another woman in the throat, not strong enough to break anything, but enough that the woman would not be able to breath properly for a while.

A rover fly stung her on the back of the head, through the fabric of her hood. It felt like a mix of fire and acid being injected into her skin. It felt bad, but had no lasting effects, so she ignored it. Pain, she could deal with.

A man swung a truncheon, too late for her to dodge. But the rovers stepped in just in time, stinging him and making him cry out, so the blow had no real force behind it.

Adelma caught it on her arm, twisted, and caught the truncheon with her free hand. She head butted the man, then kicked him in the stomach, sending him reeling back.

She held on to the truncheon, yanking it out of his grasp. Another truncheon cracked her in the back, making her grunt with pain. She whirled and smacked the woman with the truncheon straight in the cheekbone and ear. The woman went down like a sack of seagull shit.

Adelma snatched her axe from the ground and put it back in its holder at her hip. The truncheon would be a better weapon tonight. She continued with her work efficiently. The Airnians were sloppy fighters, lacking strength and discipline, so aside from a couple of stray blows and shallow cuts, Adelma took care of them relatively easily.

She collected a few stings from the rovers, too, on her hands and a couple more on her face. The pain was bad, but not unbearable, and certainly not enough to distract her. One of her eyes was starting to swell shut from a nearby sting, but she could still see well enough.

She was down to three opponents when a sharp yell tore through the air.

"Adelma!"

She spun around, very nearly getting herself skewered in the process as a woman lunged at her with a pair of twin long knives. Adelma twisted, only just avoiding the blow, which instead of stabbing her stomach, glanced over her ribs.

She hadn't noticed the second cluster of customs officers hiding in the shadows farther along from the bottleneck. Maybe Airnians weren't so stupid, in spite of their reputation. They had a wagon, and they had Kieran.

The scrawny little thing was useless in battle, and his captors were already heaving him into the wagon. Adelma cursed.

Truth be told, she wasn't particularly worried about her first mate, but she'd bought the opium using the entirety of her and her father's savings. She cared a great deal about losing that money.

With a cry, she swung her battle-axe and disarmed one of the long knives from the woman's grasp. Then she sent her forehead crashing into the woman's mouth, making her scream as blood poured out from between her teeth.

Adelma spun around, ducking away from a blow. She diverted a jab from a third man and dropped her truncheon to the ground. She punched the man square in the stomach. Adelma punched like her father—there was no quick recovery from that kind of blow.

She threw herself sideways, out of range of her final attacker, rolling back to her feet and drawing her second battle-axe again. She kicked the man she'd wounded in the head for good measure and took care of her final attacker.

By the time she made it to Kieran and the wagon, they'd managed to shackle him to the wagon's rail, and they were just beginning to leave. That was cutting it fine. Another minute or so, and she might have lost the opium.

Kieran's captors cried out, but they were even less effective than the other fighters had been. Soon enough, she had them all knocked out and on the ground.

"In the nick of time, ain't I?" Adelma grinned at Kieran, wiping sweat from her forehead with her forearm. She didn't have the patience to search the guards for the key to his shackles, and the metal chain connecting his wrists was thin enough. A well-aimed blow from her axe broke it.

"What about these?" Kieran asked sourly, waving his wrists in her face and making the remnants of the chain clink against the manacles.

"You'll get rid of them once we're back home—easy enough."

"I almost died. If you'd taken even a minute longer to get to me, I could have *died*."

Adelma put away her axes and slapped him on the back. "Oh, unclench. We're smugglers. You didn't die, so that's something to be grateful for. And now at least you got a decent story to tell people when you go to the pub back home, so cheer up."

Kieran grumbled. Adelma laughed again, clapping him on the back, and then she hauled him and the opium pack out of the wagon.

Damn, but she felt alive.

***

They were on the edge of the small coastal town, and it didn't take them long to find the delivery address. The narrow lanes they walked through could have been plucked straight out of the Rookery, if not for the lack of people—and the lack of cutthroats. The smells were essentially the same—another reminder that southern Airnia was not really that different from the Damsian Peninsula. Other than the fact that it was full of Airnians, of course.

The delivery happened smooth as paint, same as last time. Adelma performed the agreed knock, and the man who opened had the money ready. He checked the opium, and Adelma checked the coins. Everyone was professional and calm.

That was the way to do business, rather than arguing with fishwives on the docks to sell the day's catch.

Once everyone was satisfied, the man and Adelma exchanged a nod. "I'll let you know if I get my hands on more," Adelma said.

The man nodded again and shut the door. And that was that. Another smuggling job brought to successful completion.

Kieran and Adelma headed off, Adelma rubbing her hands. "Job well done… Job well done."

Once they were in another, discreet alley, she went through the coins, pocketing enough to cover what she'd spent to buy the opium in the first place. She split what was left in two equal parts.

Kieran gave her a sullen look as she handed him his money.

"What?" Adelma frowned. "You was there when I bought the opium. You know how much it cost me." She'd done that on purpose, specifically so he didn't get annoyed with the split of the money.

He shook his head. "This just ain't worth it. Not given the risks we take. This is piddly money."

"I know it ain't much, but it'll get better," Adelma replied cheerfully as she tucked her share away. "I need time to get enough cash together to be able to buy more opium at one time and get a better rate. And once people can see that I'm reliable, I'll be able to make better contacts in Damsport to smuggle for them without needing to buy the opium first. I'll figure out some other smuggling spots, and then we'll slowly make a name for ourselves." Adelma momentarily lost herself in plans and daydreams. "And then we'll start to get more interesting jobs like—"

"I ain't risking my neck further for such a pathetic amount of money."

That pulled Adelma out of her thoughts as efficiently as a kick to the arse. "*I'm* risking my neck. I do all the fighting, and you just got to keep out of the way, which you didn't even manage to do today."

"I nearly *died* today. That's risking plenty."

Adelma rolled her one good eye. "Oh, enough of that already. Nothing actually happened to you. They didn't even roughen you up. Man up already."

"You know what? You can take your bad attitude, your lack of sympathy, and shove it. I ain't doing this no more. Scrounging around in the dark for piss-poor money—I'd have better luck going back to mugging people."

Adelma frowned, more stung by the words than she would have cared to admit. Without a partner, her venture couldn't work—too many of the smuggling spots she'd figured out required two people. "And who you gonna mug? Skinny thing like you, you'd only be able to mug children."

Kieran shrugged. "I'll do what I have to do, but I ain't doing this no more."

Adelma glared at him and then threw her hands in the air. "You pathetic excuse for a first mate. You know what? I'm done with you."

"I already told you that I'm quitting."

"Oh no, you ain't—I'm throwing you out. Don't know what I were thinking putting up with such a useless excuse of a first mate. I'd be better off trying to teach an eel to knit. And you can piss off if you think you can come crying to me later, when you've failed to make a living and you're broke as a dock rat."

Adelma stomped away. Useless as Kieran was, without him, she was back to earning her living through fishing, and her dreams of becoming a proper smuggler were that much farther away.

Adelma put up her hammock in her boat, listening to the familiar sounds of the Damsian docks at night. She'd slept so often on her boat recently that she felt like she could identify the neighbouring ships simply from the creaks they made as they swayed in their berths. The sky was clear, the vast blackness punctured with stars. She crossed her arms behind her head, staring at the night sky.

Adelma wasn't the type to get dispirited, but all the same… it wasn't just that smuggling was a dream she'd had for a while now. She also needed more money than she could make just from fishing. She thought of her father and what awaited her when she got back home.

She used to love fishing, back when he was well and the two of them could roam the seas together. Now, though, everything about fishing reminded her of her Da, and when she thought of him, she couldn't help but think of what he'd been reduced to.

Adelma felt a prick of guilt at having chosen to sleep on the boat. She could have gone home and had enough time to get a little sleep before she had to leave again to fish for the day. If she didn't go home, that meant her Da wouldn't get washed today. She should really go back.

And yet she stayed in the hammock. Today was one of those days—she simply didn't have it in her to face the reality of life at the moment. Easier to stay on the boat, listening to the gentle lap of the sea against the hull. Her Da wouldn't be expecting her back, anyway, since he knew she was working tonight. Those couple extra hours of shut-eye she'd get if she stayed put were needed, too. Adelma couldn't remember the last time she'd had a full night's sleep.

But in spite of the dry, gritty tiredness she could feel in her eyes, she still couldn't sleep, and she stared at the stars instead. The thought of giving up on smuggling made her chest feel tight.

Smuggling made her feel alive, happy—free to explore. It made her feel limitless again, like when she'd first learnt sailing as a kid. She might only have been doing small runs for now, but it was a first step, until she could work up to bigger smuggling routes. And then... the world would be hers for the taking.

Her mind drifted to fishing, to the work she would have to do tomorrow, and then back to her father. She sighed and shifted in her hammock. She'd have to figure something out for the smuggling, if only to keep sane. She couldn't spend her days doing nothing more than fish, which reminded her of her old man, and then care for him at night. That wasn't a life.

His voice rang out in her mind. *The only person you can truly depend on is yourself.* He was right, of course—Kieran was proof of that. Other people were unreliable, so it wasn't a great surprise that Kieran had buggered off.

"I'll figure it out. Do it on my own if I need to," she muttered, shifting again in her hammock. Nothing was going to stop her becoming a great smuggler. Certainly not Kieran.

***

The following day, Adelma lost herself in the simple pleasure of fishing. Physical work never failed to make her feel better. She enjoyed the feel of her own strength, of her skill at sailing. The catch was good, the sun was shining, and the wind was whipping through her thick braid. In those moments, life was pretty damn fine.

And then towards the end of the day, her eyes caught onto the silver coin nailed to the mast. The reminder of her Da burst her happy bubble. She sighed, the fishing turning from joy to bitter reminder of the way things used to be.

When her attention was consumed by hard work, it was easier to ignore the signs of her father all over the boat, but now that the day was ending, they all tugged at her attention relentlessly. The silver coin nailed to the mast for favourable winds. A tiny iron anchor dangling from the tiller—touching cold iron warded off bad sea spirits.

The worst of all the superstitions, though, was the one about cats. If a cat happened to come on board, it would supposedly be a very good day, even better if the cat washed its face. Some fisherfolk, including Adelma's father, had a saucer nailed in place. He used to put out milk or food daily to entice one of the many Damsian strays on board. The damned cats pissed everywhere, stinking up the boats.

Adelma didn't have the heart to remove her father's tokens, but the cat superstition, she'd abandoned. She liked the boat to smell clean when she worked—of fish, salt, and oil.

It had been months since her Da had been well enough to come out to sea, even just to "oversee" the fishing, as he'd called it, rather than admitting he was too weak to work the nets. Adelma grimaced and rubbed the back of her neck, feeling the tension build back there. She sighed and did her best to push the thought of her father away as she finished her jobs for the day.

She set sail for the place where she currently kept her lobster pots. She and her Da had dealt with a lobster-pot thief back when she was a kid. Someone had been systematically checking their pots and emptying them. So her old man—ingenious as always—had invented a pretty amazing yet simple solution.

He'd discovered a kind of paste made from arobrum nitrate, which was sticky as a pickpocket's fingers, but slowly dissolved in seawater. He'd then had Adelma make them a new, smaller floater. It was attached by a thin bit of rope, delicate enough that it could be stuck to the side of the lobster pot using the arobrum paste.

Once the seawater had dissolved the paste, the floater was released towards the surface. For most of the day, the floater was below the water, keeping the pot safely out of sight of would-be thieves.

As Adelma reached the right spot, she found the floater. She pulled at it, feeling its smooth slick surface beneath her hands. The string below the floater was too delicate to bear the weight of the lobster pot—and hopefully of the lobster within—so instead, it was tied to a large rope. Adelma pulled the string up until she brought up the thick, sturdy rope. It was slimy with algae, and she heaved, slowly bringing the lobster pot to the surface.

Adelma cursed over and over as she saw what was inside. Not a lobster but a black-acid squid, which took up all the space so a nice juicy lobster couldn't wander in.

The squid was the size of a small cat, its body a beautifully iridescent midnight blue. It was also angry and spraying black ink everywhere. Those critters were worth a pretty penny if you could catch them, but Adelma didn't have the right equipment with her.

They were even nastier than rovers—their ink was like acid that burnt the skin real bad. Special gloves were needed to handle them. It wasn't worth her trying to catch it now—it would make a mess of her hands, and then she would have trouble working for a few days. The money alchemists paid for the ink of black-acid squids was high but not worth the loss of several days' work.

Adelma kept on cursing and swearing loudly as she went looking for something to open the lobster pot from a distance. She certainly wasn't going to do it by hand—the acidic ink was designed to work with water, so getting sprayed with ink while in the sea was nauseatingly painful.

She knew that because as a kid, she'd reached in to touch the pretty creature before her Da could warn her to keep away.

She used a pair of pliers to unhook the latch and open the back of the lobster pot. The squid swam away quickly, leaving a final—spiteful—spray of ink behind it.

"Yeah, piss off and leave my lobster pots alone," Adelma told it.

She waited a good long while for the ink to dissipate before she hauled the lobster pot in. It didn't take long for her to reset it and its floater, waiting for the paste to stick the fine string back against the trap. After a little time drying in the sun, the floater would be held securely out of sight underwater, until Adelma was back first thing the following morning.

As far as she knew, she was the only one with such a setup. Her Da had made her swear on her heart never to tell a soul.

"People ain't reliable, my girl. You think you can tell them something, and they'll keep it secret—they won't. People *always* let you down. At the end of the day, you can only rely on me and on yourself. Repeat it now, Adelma."

Adelma had dutifully repeated.

"Good. Took me a good long time to find the perfect consistency for the paste to stick proper. Can't be having no one steal our secret from us."

Adelma had never breathed a word of the lobster pots to a soul. He was a smart man, her Da. Savvy and shrewd. People always assumed big meant slow or dumb, but beneath all the brawn, her old man was sharper than a tack. Or at least he had been.

Adelma scowled at the horizon. It didn't achieve much, scowling. It wasn't like it would change things with her father. But at least it made her feel a bit better.

She continued checking the other pots. No lobsters today, but quite a few decent-sized crabs. That done, she guided the boat nimbly back to the Damsian Enclosed Docks, and it seemed that the light was somehow growing darker the closer she got. It was impossible, of course—the sun was still far from beginning its descent.

She manoeuvred the boat skilfully, feeling the familiar anger and frustration rise up. All her strength and skill as a sailor and fighter were utterly useless to make her Da right again. She was completely powerless, and she hated the feeling.

CHAPTER

3

Adelma watched as Kriss poured her a pint of weak beer. Behind the counter, the bottles of rum seemed to taunt her.

"Anyone told you that you don't look so good these days?" Kriss asked as she placed the pint down.

"You and I both know I look as rough as the wrong end of a badger." Adelma took two large gulps of beer and grimaced. "For the love of rum, this is about as good as watered-down cat's piss."

"You ordered weak beer," Kriss pointed out.

"I know. And yet you poured me a pint of cat's piss." She eyed the row of rum bottles forlornly.

"How's your Da?" Kriss asked in a low voice.

"The one-man 'death by pickling' experiment? He's doing fine." Adelma grinned, although it didn't come off quite right. It was getting harder to make flippant comments about her old man, especially when her throat tightened like it was doing at that moment.

"You know, no one's gonna judge you if you show a bit of—"

"Arse? Reckon it would shock the beer right out of everyone present."

Kriss shook her head, her eyes full of concern. "You know what I mean. You need to slow down. Feel something. You're going to run yourself into an early grave the way you're going."

"Late or early, a grave's still a grave." Her Da wanted a sea burial, when the time came...

Another patron reached the bar counter, and Kriss headed over to him, saving Adelma from having to speak. A good thing, or she might not have been able to stop her voice from wobbling.

She looked down at her pint. There was nothing to be gained by whining or throwing herself a pity party. She just did what had to be done, and that meant net fishing during the day, squid fishing at night if she couldn't get smuggling work, taking care of her Da when she wasn't working, and if she was lucky, snatching a precious few hours' sleep.

Today was a rare luxury—if drinking cat's piss could be called a luxury—although she couldn't really afford the cost of it. Her Da had asked for yet another doctor's visit, convinced he was improving.

Adelma hadn't the heart to contradict him—pain-killers didn't cure liver disease. But he wanted to see a doctor, so she got him one.

"Adelma Hensson?" a voice said at her side.

Adelma nodded without bothering to look at the doctor. They all looked the same. Neatly dressed and disapproving of her drinking. "Gotta finish my pint," she grunted.

"I have other patients, you know," the doctor said in a voice pinched with displeasure. "And I'm not sure I want to wait for the daughter of an alcoholic to finish drinking."

Adelma knocked her pint back, not wanting to risk the doctor leaving before the visit. "This way, *doctor.*"

Useless, judgemental prat. As far as she was concerned, doctors were about as useful as a barbershop on the steps of a guillotine. They just told you what you already knew and then charged exorbitant fees for it. Her Da was dying—it didn't take a medical professional to see that. He was dying, and he was getting worse by the day.

She led the prat to the house. "Here we are." She opened the door and stood aside so he could enter, not bothering to warn him about the smell.

He walked in and let out an exclamation at the stink. Adelma took a couple of deep breaths, both to get a lungful of fresh air before the putridness inside and to prepare herself for what was to come.

Her Da no longer looked like he was part of the world of the living. The stench emanating from him was so thick and cloying, every time she entered the house Adelma wanted to gag. Rot and faeces and urine. She didn't know how he could bear to sit in such filth all day every day, but he managed it somehow. The doctor looked disgusted, a handkerchief over his mouth.

"Sorry for the smell, doc," her Da said with fake cheerfulness that didn't really hide his shame. "Not got the best control of my bowels at the moment."

Jeremiah looked like a corpse. His skin was so pale and sallow, it was almost yellow. His eyes were watery and rimmed with red. Initially, he had bloated like a puffer-fish, but these days he was withered and sunken, his face little more than a skull over which his skin stretched. Adelma knew how painfully his vertebrae poked out of his back and neck. She hated the feel of them every time she washed him.

Gone was the giant, formidable man of her youth, leaving behind a small and fragile shell. Adelma watched numbly as the doctor proceeded with his examination.

"So, what's the verdict, doc?" her Da asked.

The doctor glanced at Adelma and gestured with his head towards the door. Adelma sighed and nodded, following the doctor outside. It was a relief to get a few gulps of fresh air.

"It's not good," the doctor said, shaking his head. "There's no easy way to say it…"

"He's dying," Adelma said flatly.

"Yes. Slowly, painfully, and it'll go worse before the end. It's going to be a bad death for him." The doctor at least looked genuinely sorry. "It's a real miracle that he's still alive. I've never seen anyone hold on in such a bad state. It's incredible, his organs—"

Adelma raised a hand to stop him. She already knew it all, and she didn't need to hear it again. Of course her Da was dying, and dying badly—even a deaf, blind, and dumb half-wit would be able to tell that.

"I'm sorry," the doctor said. He at least gave her a vial of something for the eye-waveringly high price of the consultation. Fat good the medication would do for a man at death's door.

She shrugged. The doctor left hurriedly, clearly relieved to get away, and Adelma returned inside.

"So? So?" her Da asked. "What did he say? I'm better, ain't I? I can feel it in my bones." He ran his fingers along his wasted arms.

Again, Adelma didn't have the heart to put him straight. It was odd—the more the illness progressed, the more feverishly convinced he became that he would somehow recover.

"He said you're a bit better, Da," she said in a low voice. He didn't even pick up on the fact that this was the first time the doctor had seen him and therefore couldn't have known how his condition compared to before.

Jeremiah rubbed his hands. "You have my potion?"

Adelma handed him the pain-killer she'd bought for him earlier, and he drank it greedily.

"It's working. I can feel it working." He smiled, his lips tinged dark purple from the potion.

"It's a pain-killer, Da," Adelma replied. Killing pain wouldn't repair the damage to his body.

"Yes, yes, but it's mighty effective. I'll get better, my girl, and when I do... When I do... Oh, we'll just see what we'll just see." He lost himself to thoughts for a time.

A spasm wracked his body, startling him. He coughed then wiped his mouth with a trembling hand, leaving a thin red smear of blood at the corner of his lips. "We'll make all this money back, my girl. I have plans, Adelma. Great plans for us both. You and me against the world, huh?" He grinned, but it came out as a grimace. "It'll be great. Don't you worry, my girl, I won't leave you alone. Your old man will keep you safe and make everything right again." Again, he lost himself in his mutterings, his mind wandering.

A fresh wave of stench announced that he'd soiled himself. Again. Adelma looked away, pretending not to have noticed, pretending not to see the pain and humiliation in his eyes.

It took a good hour to wash him. They never spoke during that time, nor did they make eye contact. Once the ordeal was over, Adelma threw open the windows, letting in some fresh air.

"Any chance of a beer for your old man?" There was a hopeful twinkle in his eye, a ghost of his old self.

Adelma smiled. "Of course." She fetched him a bottle of beer.

She knew what people said, and she didn't care. Her Da was dying, and if he wanted a beer to ease his final days, then he would have all the beer he wanted. Not only that, but if he didn't drink, he got worse. His body shook, breaking out in sweat all over, and he had terrible head and stomach aches. Better to give him enough beer on top of the pain-killer to keep him gently pickled rather than make him go through withdrawal on top of everything else.

"What about a rum chaser?" he asked, licking his lips.

Adelma shook her head. "Can't afford it, what with the doctor's fee."

"Ah… Well, never mind, my girl. We'll have all the rum we want when I'm better. Just you wait."

Adelma sat down with her head against the wall. She was far too big and too old to rest against his legs the way she used to do as a kid. But it was still nice in a nostalgic kind of way to have him in his chair and her sitting on the floor nearby. She missed the way they used to talk, missed the stories he used to tell her as a child. It really did used to feel like the two of them against the world. Now it just felt like sitting among the ruins of what used to be.

"Tell me, Da, was my Ma a good negotiator?"

He looked at her with mock wide eyes. "You mean I ain't never told you how I met your Ma?"

Adelma gave a sad smile and shook her head, re-enacting the bit they used to do when she was a kid. This had been their favourite story to share, and Adelma had always pretended she knew nothing of it.

"Oh well, my girl, ain't you in for a treat. Best story, that one. It were like this, see. One day, she came to buy my catch…"

Adelma leaned her head back against the wall, closing her eyes and wondering how many more times her Da would tell that story. This moment of the day was the best for him, when he had a beer and he got to lose himself in his memories. A little of his old vitality returned for those few moments, and they could almost pretend things were back to normal.

Once he was done telling the story of how he'd met her mother, he told the story of the first time he took Adelma drinking when she was young. How she'd thrown up in the street, getting it all over her long black hair. Adelma had shaved the sides of her head the following morning—and she'd done it badly, cutting the skin and leaving tufts of hair sticking out—so that if she threw up again, her hair couldn't get in the way. Damn if her old man hadn't almost dissolved with pride at her determination to try drinking again.

Then he told the story of the first time he'd bought her knuckle dusters to help her take care of bullies who were picking on her. That was a good one, and Adelma smiled as her Da described just how she'd knocked out a boy twice her size with a single blow.

As she did most nights, Adelma sent up a silent prayer, hoping some god somewhere was listening. She asked that tonight, sleep would take her Da quietly and painlessly.

CHAPTER

4

There were all kinds of different pubs in Damsport. Choosing one depended on what you were after, and what kind of person you wanted to see. There were brawling pubs, where you went if you were looking for a fight; cross-eyed pubs, where the booze was dirty, cheap, and had you clinging to the floor to stop yourself from falling in under an hour; pubs that specialised in certain kinds of beers or ciders or other alcohols; pubs that only served rum; pubs to pick up female prostitutes; and pubs to pick up male prostitutes.

Today, Adelma wanted to have a drink at the Rising Kraken. It had been six months since her Da had passed. For all that she'd tried, she hadn't managed to scrounge even the smallest smuggling job since Kieran had left. And the debts she'd accumulated in the final months of her Da's life had been too pressing to allow her the luxury of spare time. But now that her debts were finally wiped, she had a little money in her pocket, and most importantly, she had the time to invest in networking and making contacts.

It was time to get back to her dreams of becoming a smuggler, and the stars were aligning in an unbelievably perfect way. The Widow, who ran the largest gang in Damsport and the most important smuggling ring, was looking for new smugglers to join her operation. The recruitment drive was taking place in the morning. So for tonight, Adelma wanted to treat herself.

This was going to be her very first visit to the Rising Kraken. The place was expensive—a serious cut above the places she was used to drinking in. She'd grown up among the roughest, dirtiest pubs in Damsport. Compared to that, the Rising Kraken was so posh, she might as well be entering the Marchioness's Mansion.

The Rising Kraken, however, was a favourite among the well-established smugglers and, more importantly, among their clients and suppliers. In short, it was the place to go to make contacts and move up in that world. Adelma wasn't expecting to pick up a new client tonight, but it would be good to get to know the faces of a few of the more important smugglers, maybe even chat with one or two.

She pushed the door open and stopped in her tracks as she caught sight of the ceiling. Rippling, shimmering blue light cast patterns that perfectly replicated sunlight playing on the surface of the sea. It was disorientating at first, especially since the rest of the lighting was low and the floor was dark. It created the impression of having stepped into an otherworldly place deep beneath the sea. In the middle of the main room, a large shadow had been painted on the ceiling in the shape of a kraken. It loomed over the place, the rippling blue light playing over its body.

An ankle-deep layer of alchemical mist covered the ground so that Adelma couldn't see what she was stepping on. Brittle things crunched underfoot. Possibly bits of seashells, since this was a posh place. In the places she was used to, it would have been old peanut shells.

The tables weren't scuffed with age and bad treatment, but instead polished to a shine. A small boat's hull had been repurposed to make the bar, a beautifully painted kraken tentacle extending across it. A mirror gave the impression that a second room skulked behind the counter. A pleasant aroma of spiced rum wafted about the place, welcoming Adelma and enticing her to have a drink. She would be glad to oblige.

As she grabbed a high stool at the bar, she did a quick sweep of the room, feeling pleased. No one seemed to stare at her for being out of place.

She glanced at herself in the mirror. The sides of her head were shaved, leaving a thick braid of hair along the top and back that reached all the way to her waist. Her skin had the dark, weather-beaten look that spoke of a sailor living at sea. Her hands were strong and thickly jointed, her limbs and torso covered with hard muscle that showed beneath her shirt.

In short, she looked like she belonged here. The thought made her grin. She was a damned good sailor, and she was smart enough to figure out smuggling routes. She'd make a great smuggler—she just needed to get a proper start.

She was about to order herself a shot of rum when a man entered the bar, catching her attention. He was bigger than her, which always made her take notice. Few people matched her in size, and fewer still were taller.

His paddle-sized, square hands had HOLD FAST tattooed across his thick knuckles. His skin also had the dark look of a man living at sea, and his black hair was shaved to a dark fuzz. Tattoos were scattered up his forearms, disappearing under the rolled-up sleeves of his loose white shirt. And it was a crisp white—not the faded, old-tooth yellow, which was the way white clothing normally went out at sea.

Adelma watched Hold Fast appreciatively in the mirror as he slid into a nearby booth, opposite another man. He moved well.

"Heard you ran into a spot of bother," the man said.

Hold Fast gave a wry laugh, shaking his head. "Sparkles, man. Made the meet, though."

Adelma ordered herself a shot of rum. Smugglers had their own language, and she didn't know what "sparkles" stood for. The meet was the delivery—that much she knew. She would have to learn the language, like entering a secret society.

She glanced up into the mirror again, to find Hold Fast looking at her. He gave her a quick grin and a wink before turning back to his conversation.

Adelma sipped her rum. It was good stuff. Seriously good stuff. Liquid gold, her Da would have said. He would be proud to see her now—having worked off all her debts and making a new life for herself. The thought pulled a curtain of sadness over her thoughts.

She ordered herself another rum and found herself reminiscing over some of her favourite memories of him, back when he was strong and healthy.

She understood now, why her Da had told the same stories over and over again at the end. There was something comforting about losing herself in the familiar trails of the past. She thought of one of his favourites—the first time he'd bought her brass knuckles, teaching her how to retaliate against the bullies who found it amusing to beat up the big, awkward girl. *Always come back harder and faster than they'd expect, my girl. Never leave an uneven score.*

And hadn't she given the bullies a shock. Broken some noses and knocked out some teeth, she had. And her old man proud as punch. Adelma was horrified to realise her eyes had filled with tears, and she wiped them angrily.

What the hell am I doing? The absolute last thing she needed tonight was to make a spectacle of herself among the smuggler crowd. What if the Widow heard of it? Strong, no nonsense, capable—that was the kind of woman who got hired by the Widow, not some tragic basket case crying at the bar.

"Well, look at that! A freak escaped from the freak show!"

Adelma was yanked out of her thoughts. The man who had spoken was walking past, with a foreigner in tow. Clearly drunk, he had the dark colouring of a Damsian, and he looked vaguely familiar. That was as far as Adelma got before a rapidly growing red mist of anger overtook her thoughts.

"Oh, it's looking at me. It's looking at me," the Damsian man said, coming to a halt. "Screw me sideways, it's uglier when I see it fully frontal. Mariano, have you ever seen such a beast? It's like a cow mated with a, a… Mariano, you'll have to accept my apologies. I wasn't planning on forcing you to look at the dregs of Damsian—"

Always come back harder and faster than they'd expect. Adelma interrupted him with a lightning-quick punch to the temple—her signature move, which she used any time someone was stupid enough to insult her within punching range. The man collapsed as clumsily as innards falling out of a gutted fish, banging his head again on the floor. The alchemical mist swirled around him.

Adelma took a step towards the foreigner, who regarded her calmly. "I don't like pretty boys, and I don't like people what listen to their mates insulting me," she told him.

She slapped him open-handed, hard enough to make him stagger back. She saw two men coming towards her out of the corner of her eye. They had the look of paid muscle, and Adelma realised the foreigner was dressed very expensively. The kind of man who was likely to hire bodyguards.

Bring it on. Adelma felt ready to take on everyone in the pub. Hell, she felt ready to take on everyone in Damsport, everyone the world, for that matter.

She reached for her axes, then strong hands grabbed her and yanked her towards the door.

"What the hell?" Adelma tried to jerk herself free, but the man holding her was too strong. It was Hold Fast.

"What you doing?" she snarled.

"Saving your skin." Hold Fast's voice was a low, smooth rumble as they stepped outside.

"Let go of me. I'm perfectly capable of seeing to my own skin."

"D'you know who you hit?"

"A prat who deserved it."

Hold Fast led the way to a quiet side street and finally let go of her. By some miracle of restraint, Adelma didn't headbutt him there and then.

"So you don't know who you hit," he said.

"I told you—a prat who deserved it."

Hold Fast grinned, his smile lighting up his face. "Can't disagree with you there. But much as it was fun watching Assurak get his arse handed to him, I couldn't let you dig yourself a deeper hole. I've seen you around. You've been trying to set yourself up as a smuggler, ain't you? Interesting strategy to knock out one of the Widow's top lieutenants—even if he did deserve it."

Adelma groaned. Assurak. She knew the name, and now she knew why he'd looked familiar. And the day before the Widow's recruitment drive, too. The fight went out of her as abruptly as it had come. She cursed repeatedly.

"Ah. You were planning to join the Widow's crew tomorrow at the recruitment drive," Hold Fast guessed.

Adelma nodded, her anger growing again. "If that arsewipe had kept his mouth shut, all would still be fine." *Never leave an uneven score,* her Da reminded her.

"The man's an arse, no doubt about it. But it might also be an idea to check who you're dealing with before you knock their lights out," Hold Fast said.

"Don't lecture me."

"I mean, don't get me wrong, I'd have punched him too, if I was you. I'm Tom Riddick, by the way, although everyone calls me Radish." He rubbed a hand over his bald head. "Probably on account of my size."

That drew a snort from Adelma. "Yeah, you're almost as small as I am."

Radish laughed. "I am, at that. Only a few inches taller than you. What's your name then?"

"Adelma. No nickname."

Radish was somehow managing to dispel her anger a little. Something about his easy smile, maybe. "Well, Adelma no nickname, I'd stay clear of the Kraken for a little while. Mariano's one of Assurak's top clients, and you'll have completely humiliated Assurak in front of him. And for tomorrow—well, Assurak can hold a grudge like nobody's business."

"So can I."

"You sound proud of that."

"I am, as it goes—my old man was the same. Although it ain't so much that we hold grudges, and more that we always pay back someone what does us wrong."

"Not sure that's such a good idea with Assurak. Give him time to cool off. Lie low, avoid the recruitment drive tomorrow, and—"

Adelma frowned at him. "What exactly gave you the idea that I'm in the market for advice? I can look after myself, and I don't need you riding to the rescue."

Radish gave a wry smile and put his hands up. "Alright. You strike me as a pretty capable woman."

"Good. Because I know what I'm doing." Adelma's frustration with the evening was surging up again.

Radish, on the other hand, was so relaxed, it was oozing from his pores. It was odd—Adelma was used to people growing stiff or annoyed when she rejected them.

"Well, since that's cleared up, fancy a drink?" His eyes twinkled.

Adelma shook her head, even though a small part of her was tempted, and she made a point of not normally passing up on a free drink. But she didn't feel like being sociable. "Thanks, but I'll just call it a night. I want to be up early for the meeting tomorrow."

"You still gonna go to the Widow?"

"Damn right. Way I see, Assurak and I are even now. He insulted me, and I hit him. Fair's fair, and he ain't got no reason to be pissed at me."

"He might not see it that way." Radish must have read the change in Adelma's face, because he laughed and put his hands up again. "I weren't giving you advice. You do you. See you around, Adelma no nickname." He touched two fingers to his forehead and walked off.

Adelma watched him leave, frowning. Maybe she would bear in mind that Assurak was likely to be angry at her in the morning when she showed up. But if Adelma explained the whole encounter to the Widow, the woman was sure to side with Adelma. In fact, Adelma felt quite confident that no one would think she was in the wrong for decking Assurak tonight.

Adelma continued to mull this over as she headed home. "I mean, what if I'd been a potential client and that moron had insulted me?" she muttered to herself. "What if I were someone with real business potential for the Widow?" Adelma shook her head to herself.

By the time she reached home, she was completely confident in her position, and sure she would be able to explain away any objections the Widow might have.

The following morning, Adelma awoke feeling bright and excited. She stropped her cut-throat razor and carefully scraped the sides of her head so they would look nice and neat. That done, she loosened her plait and re-braided it.

Once she was ready, she headed to Bayog, one of the more unsavoury parts of Damsport. It was the kind of place where sane, rational people entered, and dribbling fools left, unable to tell their arses from their foreheads. Adelma was actually quite fond of the area. It was remarkably well organised, all things considered. The gambling dens, brothels, opium parlours, and drinking holes were helpfully clustered in such a way that, if the cards were generous, punters could spank their winnings on their favourite vice, or they could find a comforting spot to drown their sorrows. No matter the game, no matter the vice, the biggest winners in Bayog were those lining the pockets of the Widow.

Adelma passed a few Nightingales who were either finishing up for the day or plying the somewhat less profitable daytime trade. Nightingales were the exclusive gang of prostitutes who worked Bayog, and it had been a long time since anyone had been fool enough to step in on their turf. Even the Widow gave them a wide berth.

Adelma nodded respectfully to one of them as she walked past. The prostitute's makeup was greasy, the heavy black kohl smeared from her lids to form dark, smudged circles around her eyes. Her breasts strained against her corset, and it was a marvel both of engineering and gravity that they hadn't yet popped out. She was also armed to the teeth.

Adelma reached the area specialising in opium, picking her way over the opium wraiths who lay slack jawed in the gutter, staring at the sky. The Widow's compound was just around the corner, and Adelma felt her excitement rising.

She wondered how soon she would be given a job. Initially, it would be something small, smuggling goods of little value as they tested out her skills, which was fine. She'd outshine all the others and quickly become indispensable. And then... Then the world would be hers for the taking.

Adelma knocked at the door.

***

The search Adelma was subjected to was thorough in the extreme.

"Easy, boy," she told the man patting her down. "I normally like a few drinks before getting so intimate."

The man ignored her.

"I ain't got another battle-axe smuggled up my arse, in case you were wondering. Or anywhere else, for that matter," Adelma added as he removed the two she had at her hips. The man didn't so much as quirk a smile. *Tough crowd.*

The man finished searching her. "She's clean," he grunted.

"Didn't you *hear* any of the jokes I made just now?" she replied.

The second guard gave a little snort of laughter. They were both big, probably in order to intimidate, but that didn't work on someone like Adelma. She was enjoying being among people her own size for once.

The search over, she was taken down a long corridor dotted with doors. They passed a room with a wall made of slate atop which a myriad of numbers were scrawled—odds on bets. People were streaming in and out through a door at the back of the room, depositing money with the bookies, all women. Their white shirt sleeves were hiked up and kept in place by copper cuffs just above their elbows, and their voices were loud and efficient. Cigar smoke wafted out, smelling of burnt grass and dark chocolate.

The next room Adelma passed contained four men so beefy, they made the room look cramped, and they supervised as two significantly smaller men carefully counted and weighed out coins. A typist noted everything down with clacks of his typewriter. The next few doors were ominously closed, but dull thudding could be heard through one of them.

"In here." One of the men ushered Adelma through an open doorway.

Inside was a windowless room wall-papered with maps. A number of shipping routes were drawn out—the official routes the Widow's operations would be covering as part of her legitimate trading operations. Any smuggling routes would, of course, be kept under wraps.

A desk faced the room. At a smaller table next to it, a typist sat, looking bored. A handful of men and women were already waiting. Alchemical globes with heavy lampshades hung from the ceiling, so everyone's face was illuminated from above, creating deep shadows beneath their cheekbones and in their eye sockets.

Some of the people waiting looked nervous, and with good reason. Rumours abounded about the Widow, whose full name was actually Widow Bones. Nobody really knew if Bones was her real name, or if she had even ever had a husband. Some said she was called the Widow because of all the widows she'd created over the years, killing off men who had lost at her gambling tables and couldn't pay. Others claimed she'd had her husband killed in varying shudder-inducing ways, when he'd gotten in the way of her business.

There was the story that she'd hired an assassin to poison all her rivals, and the story of how she dealt with a mole within her organisation—no one really knew what had been done to the mole to mangle her body that badly. Whether the rumours were true or not, one thing was clear: you didn't mess with the Widow.

The tension in the air thickened as more and more people arrived, sizing each other up. Adelma smirked at the sideways glances she received. She looked like she meant business, and she was feeling good.

Da will be proud when I tell him... Disappointed that I'm dropping the fishing, but then—

Adelma caught herself as she realised she was picturing recounting the day's events to her old man that evening. *Really not the time to get emotional.*

A commotion at the entrance yanked her out of her thoughts.

"Form a line," one of the guards at the door called out.

Adelma found herself at the front of the queue. Voices drifted over through the open door, along with footsteps and the sound of laughter. A small group entered the room, led by a man with shiny, slicked-back black hair. Adelma hadn't noticed the hair last night, but she definitely recognised the nasty black eye.

Assurak started at the sight of her. Then a sly look crept into his eyes, and he murmured something to one of the men walking with him. Adelma felt a hot flush of anger creeping up her neck. She knew whatever had been said was about her, and she had to swallow down the urge to step forward and confront them.

Assurak sat behind the desk. "My name is Assurak," he announced in a clear voice. "The Widow has charged me to vet you sorry lot and to select a short list for her to consider as potential new joiners for her network."

Adelma's stomach sank. She'd expected to be able to speak to the Widow in person, to explain anything that needed explaining.

Assurak looked down and opened a ledger atop the desk, making a "come here" gesture with two fingers to indicate that Adelma should step forward. She gritted her teeth and obeyed. She felt angry at herself for being so bloody naive in thinking she would be able to explain herself to the Widow. *Stupid, stupid, stupid.*

"Name?" Assurak asked, still without looking at her.

"Adelma Hensson."

He looked up and pretended to look surprised. "Bugger me sideways, you're an ugly one."

"Didn't realise the Widow were running a beauty pageant," Adelma replied.

"No, but I doubt she'd want to have to look at your nasty mug every day."

"She won't have to if I'm off smuggling for her. I'll be at sea."

"Hmmm." Assurak pretended to consider. "Problem with someone as big as you is that you're easy to spot. Smugglers need to be discrete."

"Ships are bigger than people."

"Can you even sail?" Assurak asked.

"Been sailing since I were old enough to walk. My old man was a fisherman, and—"

"We don't take on fisherfolk," Assurak interrupted. He smiled nastily and waved a dismissal.

Adelma glared at him. "If this is about last night, you are I are even now, alright? You insulted me and—"

"I said we don't take on fisherfolk," Assurak said loudly. "Are you deaf? Or are you stupid? Must be all the empty space in that massive skull of yours. Next in line."

"You heard him," one of the guards grunted, moving closer to Adelma. The meaning was clear—move or be moved.

Nothing had ever cost Adelma so much as moving aside. She was outnumbered and out-weaponed, so she had no choice but to do as she was told. And starting up a fight in the Widow's compound would be a whole other level of stupid.

The next man in line approached the desk, obviously nervous, holding his hat in his hands. "I'm also a fisherman, but I've been doing small smuggling runs on the side, and—"

Assurak waved a hand, interrupting him. "Excellent. We need good sailors."

Adelma watched, rage welling up inside her. If Assurak thought he could mess with her dreams and get away with it, he was utterly deluded. He was going to pay for this, and with interest. *High* interest.

Come back at them harder and faster than they expect. And she would do just that.

CHAPTER 6

Getting even was all well and good, but it didn't put food on the table, and it wasn't going to help Adelma become a smuggler, either. She decided she'd been approaching things the wrong way. Much as she loved the idea of running her own routes, maybe trying to get work aboard a smuggler's ship, among a larger crew, was more realistic for now.

It would be a way to earn a living other than fishing, allowing her to build contacts and get experience. Of course there might be trouble when the time came to set herself up as an independent, but she would have to cross that bridge when she came to it.

She'd identified a few smugglers here and there over the last few months, and she decided that the following morning she would approach them—the rest of the day was going to have to be spent fishing. She didn't have many contacts, but they might be able to point her in the direction of someone looking for a decent sailor to join their crew.

The first smuggler she approached told her he had no work. No great surprise—she hadn't expected to score a win on her first try. He also couldn't give her advice as to where to look.

The next also had no work, and then the third. The fourth was a grizzled woman who stank of gin and chewed some kind of tobacco that turned her spit black. She spat out a thick glob as Adelma asked about work.

"Work, eh? You can sail?" the smuggler asked.

Adelma nodded. "Da was a fisherman. Grew up on his boat."

"You know the new steam engines?"

"Yep," Adelma lied. *How hard can it be? Can't be harder than figuring out the winds, and I've got those licked.*

The smuggler nodded, chewing her tobacco thoughtfully. "Name?"

"Adelma. Adelma Hensson."

The smuggler looked up sharply. "Sorry," she grunted. "No work."

Suspicion dawned on Adelma. "Has someone been to see you? Told you not to give me work?" A flash of guilt in the woman's eyes told Adelma all she needed to know. "It were Assurak, weren't it?" she asked in a low voice. "I know it. At least do me the favour of confirming it."

The smuggler grimaced and then nodded grudgingly. "He's too close to the Widow. Can't afford to get on his wrong side." She sighed. "I'm sorry, girl. You seem a decent sort. Whatever you did to piss him off, it's gonna follow you. That man never lets go of a grudge."

"Neither do I," Adelma replied darkly.

The smuggler had been right, though—Assurak had been thorough. She tried the last few smugglers she knew of, but she couldn't even find work as a deckhand. They all turned her away. Some sent her packing before she even opened her mouth, probably recognising her, given how distinctive she was.

Adelma guessed that if she were to ask every single smuggler in Damsport, she would find that Assurak had ensured no one would touch her with a ten-foot pole. She decided to leave the docks before she did something stupid, like headbutt someone. She really needed to hit something, and it was getting harder to keep that under control.

As she headed off, she passed a ship whose captain was in the middle of an argument with a dockmistress. The ship looked ready to be tied to the dock, but the dockmistress and her workers were clearly preventing that from happening.

"Rules are the rules," the dockmistress said. "You got to go to the quarantine area."

"But it's nothing lethal," the captain protested. Adelma recognised him—Lukas was his name. She'd had a few drinks with him here and there over the years.

"It's just the stomach flu or something like that!" Lukas shouted at the dockmistress from the ship.

The dockmistress crossed her arms. "Let me make myself perfectly clear: either you sail over to the quarantine area by yourself, or I'll have your ship dragged over, and you will face investigation for attempting to bring disease into the city."

The vein on Lukas's forehead looked like it might burst.

At least there was someone who was having a worse day than Adelma. Ships that carried disease, or that were suspected of carrying disease, had to remain in the quarantine area, a small system of floating docks set up immediately within the walls of the Damsian Enclosed Docks. The ship would have to remain there for forty days, to ensure the sickness had passed.

Adelma had seen the quarantine area, and she could understand Lukas's reticence at spending forty days there—it was really far from pleasant. But she could also understand why the dockmistress didn't want to let a ship dock if it was carrying some kind of stomach flu.

"Lukas," she called, waving.

"Adelma, hey. Talk some sense into her, would you?" He gestured at the dockmistress.

"Come on, get sense knocked into *your* head, Lukas. Ain't no one wants to catch your arse-spraying mayhem. Go to the quarantine area."

"Don't bloody start, you." Lukas pointed a finger at her, apparently in short supply of humour, which was understandable. He turned back to the dockmistress. "Look, get a doctor on board to come and examine my man. Maybe it's not even stomach flu. Maybe it's food poisoning. Maybe... I don't know, dammit. I'm no doctor!"

Adelma left him to it and headed to the Old Girl's Arms. It was still a bit early in the day for fights to be going on, but that might change, and she might need to burn off some of her frustration with Assurak.

The pub was as grotty as ever. Sawdust covered the floor, the fresh layer not enough to mask the smells of the night before. The high metal stools at the counter were screwed to the floor so they couldn't be thrown around. Punters had to bring their own tankards or buy one before drinking. In short, there was nothing to break, nothing to damage, and the barkeep made herself scarce at the first sign of trouble.

"Kriss, you beauty," Adelma grunted as she slid herself onto a stool. "Have I told you how marvellously generous and kind you look, polishing that tankard?"

Kriss raised an eyebrow. "You forgot your tankard again, didn't you?"

Kriss had only recently taken over running the Arms from her mother. She was in her early twenties, a few years younger than Adelma. A lean young woman with dark skin, quick eyes, she had the tendency to raise an eyebrow when she didn't approve of something.

Adelma grinned. "Guilty. But on account of all that generosity oozing out your pores, I figured you might be persuaded to loan me one? I'm too skint to buy one."

Kriss's eyebrow arched higher.

"Your eyebrow's trying to migrate to your hairline," Adelma said innocently.

"Hmm."

"Come on, Kriss. It's been a bad day." She explained about Assurak.

Kriss sighed. "I'm too nice for my own good." She slid a full tankard of beer across the counter. "On the house, ale and all."

"You are a goddess among women." Adelma savoured the first sip of ale, so thick and dark she could almost chew it. "Nobody makes ale as good as you."

"Damn right." Kriss returned to pottering behind the bar, looking pleased. Adelma lost herself in her thoughts, which had shot back to smuggling and Assurak with all the speed of a homing pigeon.

She had to assume that Assurak had effectively closed Damsport's smuggling circles to her, which meant she had two options: leave Damsport and try to set herself up somewhere else or find a way to batter down the door. Adelma frowned. Leaving Damsport felt like admitting defeat. Her Da would never have stood for that. In fact, he would probably already be battering down the door.

Adelma chewed that idea over. What would battering down the door look like? *Going straight to the Widow, that's what. And why not?* The Widow was a business woman, and if Adelma made her an offer too good to turn down, the Widow wasn't going to care about Assurak's vendetta.

Adelma downed her pint and slammed it on the counter. She hadn't the foggiest idea of what could get the Widow so interested, but no matter. That kind of detail wasn't going to stop her. If she got employment directly from the Widow, all the other smugglers would piss on Assurak's black mark against her.

And then Adelma would make Assurak truly rue the day he'd insulted her.

"I swear, I ain't never seen you so thoughtful," Kriss said. "Although now you look like you're about to punch someone."

"I am at that. I need to figure out how to take Assurak down."

Kriss shook her head. "Only you could turn becoming a smuggler into some kind of personal battle."

Adelma frowned. "What d'you mean?"

"That you take after your old man."

Adelma smiled at the compliment.

"Have you considered trying to have a bit of a nice time?" Kriss asked. "You know, have some fun. Live a little."

"What you on about? I live plenty."

"I mean be a bit more sociable. Enjoy yourself."

"Enjoy myself? I'm enjoying myself plenty. I got a pint of ale, I got my plans, and I got you to talk to, when you ain't busting my chops about having fun."

"So you wouldn't say no to a bit of good time?" Kriss asked.

Adelma sighed. "What are you on about, woman? Spit it out already."

Kriss cocked her head. "I'm talking about strapping young lads."

Adelma snorted. "Strapping? A 'strapping' lad is too small for the likes of me."

"Would I qualify as strapping?" a male voice said next to her.

Adelma started and turned to find Radish leaning against the bar. He grinned. "I might be a bit too old to be called a lad, though, seeing as I'm gonna turn forty in a couple years."

"I reckon you totally qualify as strapping," Kriss said. "Adelma's kind of strapping, in fact."

"Huh, good to know." Radish's smile turned even more broad.

Adelma glared at Kriss.

"And we was just saying that Adelma needs to get out more," Kriss continued. "You know, be sociable."

"Ain't you got a tankard to polish?" Adelma asked her pointedly.

"I just like to look out for my customers," Kriss said innocently.

Radish turned to Adelma. "How about a drink? Maybe not here—don't want to get drawn into a fight or nothing. But the Hand and Tankard down the road's nice enough."

"I'm fine here. Kriss was just about to pour me another pint."

"Actually…" Kriss said.

Adelma gave her a dangerous look. "I said I'm fine here."

"Hmm, yes, except that I'm all out of ale," Kris said.

"We both know that's utter rubbish," Adelma said. "Anyway, you can pour me some beer or some rum instead. And don't tell me you've run out of rum, because I can see it in the bottles behind you."

Kriss shook her head. "Display merchandise only. Bottles are full of dark cane juice. Not a drop of rum in the joint." She sighed, putting on a regretful expression. "Times are tough, and I'm all out of stock. Reckon you'd best take the offer from the strapping lad if you want another drink." She winked at Radish.

Adelma rolled her eyes. "The subtlety is making me feel like someone just hit me in the head with a brick."

"Anything less than that, and you wouldn't pick up on it," Kriss said, eyes dancing with amusement. "I know because I've tried."

"So," Radish said. "Hand and Tankard?"

Adelma let out a suffering sigh. "Seems I have no choice, do I?"

Radish looked over at Kriss. "Don't she just know how to make a strapping lad feel special?"

CHAPTER

The Hand and Tankard was a cosy pub, with lots of old, well-worn tables, and chairs with seats polished smooth by the thousands of arses that had sat on them before. The furniture was a mishmash of stolen, recycled, and made by the owner, and none of the chairs were the right height for the tables.

The table Radish selected looked more like a coffee table next to the chairs surrounding it. The surface was flat, though, and drinks could be placed on it, so it was absolutely fine in Adelma's book.

"What's your poison?" Radish asked.

Adelma chose a rum, and Radish returned with two glasses of spicy-smelling amber liquid.

"Heard about the stunt Assurak pulled, by the way." He shook his head. "Sorry about that. I've never agreed with black marks being placed on people. That's real bad. In your case 'specially, given how Assurak behaved before."

Adelma nodded, taking a sip of her rum. She could feel something loosen inside of her. She would never have admitted to it, but it felt soothing to have someone else agree that the situation was unfair. She would have been even less likely to admit this, but sometimes taking on the whole world by herself was tiring. And lonely.

"Normally, I'd have offered you a place on my ship," Radish said. "Assurak's pettiness can piss up a mast far as I'm concerned, but I got no ship at the moment."

"A smuggler with no ship?" Adelma asked, frowning.

Radish smiled, looking utterly unconcerned. "I took a big gamble, and it didn't work out. Lost my ship and my cargo into the bargain."

"Shouldn't you be a bit more upset or worried?" For Adelma, losing her Da's ship would be beyond devastating. She couldn't even fathom what life would be like without it. That ship was what made her still feel connected to him. It made her feel less alone and freakish in the world.

"Nah, no need to be upset," Radish replied. "Wouldn't achieve none. Anyway, I'm considering giving up the life."

"Smuggling? Why on earth would you do that?"

Radish shrugged. "I ain't completely sure yet. Maybe when I get my ship back, I'll feel different. She'll be back where she belongs soon enough."

Adelma gave a little smile at the warmth in Radish's voice when he'd spoken about his ship. That, she could understand. That feeling that your ship was a person in some way.

"So what d'you smuggle?" Adelma asked.

"Whatever pays. Mostly swish these days—I'm real good at getting past booze blockades. But I'll do the luxury runs for tax evasion, some dream deliveries, some—"

"Dream pays well for you?" Adelma asked. Dream was opium. Expensive to buy without the right contacts, which then made smuggling it real poor business, as she'd found out with Kieran.

"Very."

Adelma felt a rush of envy. Radish was so casual about it, but months of hard work hadn't been enough for Adelma to make opium smuggling profitable. He clearly had some really good contacts.

It suddenly occurred to her that a golden opportunity had dropped right into her lap: a well-established smuggler who seemed happy enough to share information, and who wasn't bothered by Assurak's black mark. No point asking for work, considering what he'd just said about giving up smuggling. Information, though, could be just as valuable.

"What's the most risky route?" she asked instead. "The one no one wants to do, not for any money?"

"Teraverre," he said right away, with an easy smile. "For opium, that is. No one's ever managed to smuggle it there, so for now, it ain't even a route."

Adelma's interest was immediately pricked. *Just the kind of thing that would convince the Widow to hire me.* Smuggling opium into Teraverre would establish her as someone to be taken seriously.

"Only way in is through the customs funnel," Radish continued, "and those bastards are the best I've ever encountered. They can smell hidden cargo. If they find any dream in your ship, that's you with a second smile, going overboard."

Adelma's eyebrows shot up. "Seriously? You mean—"

Radish ran a finger across his neck.

"Damn."

"Yeah. That's why nobody wants to take opium there. Too much risk."

Adelma did all she could to keep her excitement under wraps. Smuggling opium into Teraverre would definitely get the Widow's attention. Of course there was the matter of figuring out how to do that in the first place. But if there was one thing Adelma trusted fully, it was her ability to get things done. And it should give her enough clout to *crush* Assurak. She felt a vicious sense of vindication at the thought of evening out that score.

Radish began to recount an amusing anecdote from one of his booze blockade runs, his voice a smooth, deep rumble. Adelma pushed the thoughts of smuggling opium to Teraverre away for now, not wanting to risk letting on what she was thinking.

Radish finished his story, and Adelma laughed at the punch line. It reminded her of an incident on her boat with her father, and she recounted it. Radish then added another one of his stories, and then another. He was a good story-teller, setting the scene and doing good impressions, and he had a good sense of humour.

For a time, Adelma forgot about everything, losing herself in Radish's tales of adventures at sea and crime on shore, his deep voice drawing her in. His was just the life she wanted for herself.

Adelma realised she had finished her rum, and she surprised herself by offering to buy them another round.

"Sure," Radish replied with a smile.

Adelma headed back to the bar, and as she walked away from Radish, it was as though a spell lifted, leaving her with a profound sense of unease. She glanced back at him, but he wasn't looking at her. Radish appeared perfectly relaxed, which seemed to be his default setting, from what she could tell. Adelma reviewed their conversation as she ordered the two rums, trying to figure out what had unsettled her.

It wasn't until the barkeep returned with two glasses of golden liquid that it hit her. She had no idea what Radish was after. Why had he come looking for her at the Old Girl's Arms? And why invite her for a drink?

Everyone was always after something—the men even more so. They wanted to goad her into a fight to see what it would be like to wrestle with a beast like her. They wanted to impress their friends or follow through on a dare. They wanted to set her up to be made a joke of. Sometimes they also just wanted to sleep with her, for the same reasons as for the fighting.

But she couldn't read anything on Radish. He didn't seem to be after anything, or if he was, he was hiding it better than anyone ever had. She'd dropped her guard as they'd talked, letting the stories lull her into relaxing.

Adelma returned with the two rums, determined not to let that happen again. Radish was after something, and she would figure out what. Was he being nice to her because he wanted an ally against Assurak? Did he want access to her boat, since he'd lost his?

She handed Radish his rum and plonked herself back on her chair. "So," she said without preamble, "you got something against Assurak?"

Radish raised an eyebrow. "Assurak? Not really. But then I don't associate with pricks."

"Here's to that," Adelma said, raising her drink. She sipped her rum and observed Radish over her glass. "So you in the market for a new ship? Looking for someone to front you a boat?"

Radish quirked a smile. "Nah. I've got a plan. It'll take me some time, but I'll get my lady back. Until then, I don't mind being landlocked. Like I said, I'm considering giving up the life anyway."

He continued talking easily. This time, Adelma didn't let him get to her with his stories and his deep, rumbly voice. He didn't have the jumpiness of someone on a dare to take her to bed. There was no aggression to him, so he clearly wasn't after a fight. He was drinking slowly, so he wasn't trying to pit his drinking abilities against hers, another thing that happened often. And he didn't seem to be the kind to set up an elaborate prank—like the time she'd been caught up in conversation, only to have her interlocutor's friends arrange for a bucket of fish guts to be dropped on her.

She'd been fifteen back then. Still naive. But she'd gotten her own back, as she always did. There'd been a bad mugging. The lad she'd been talking to had lost all his front teeth, so he now lisped in a ridiculous manner. Of the other two, one now had a useless, mangled left hand, and the other a limp.

Nobody knew who the violent mugger was, but the three lads had grown rather afraid of Adelma after that. They had never come near her again. A wise decision.

Adelma turned her attention back to Radish, still trying to guess his motives. The conversation flowed on easily, and it wasn't until he stood up, announcing that it was his round that she realised that her glass was empty again. Determined to figure out his angle, Adelma agreed to another drink.

Radish headed to the bar, moving like he had all the time in the world. Adelma had rarely seen anyone who projected such an unhurried, calm aura. He was completely different from everyone she'd met, and she didn't like it. Different meant unpredictable, and she liked being able to anticipate trouble before it hit.

She did, however, enjoy watching him walk to the bar. Beneath the calm was real strength—something Adelma very much appreciated. Muscle rolled beneath his dark skin, to be guessed at under the loose white shirt. And he looked even better from the front, grinning at her as he returned with their rums, a wiry thatch of chest hair visible at the shirt's wide opening.

So what's his angle?

***

Three rums later, Adelma's confusion about Radish's lack of ulterior motives had turned to frustration. She'd gradually eliminated all possibilities and decided it had to be that he wanted to take her to bed. Something that she wouldn't mind, actually.

He was, however, taking his damned time about it, and Adelma was losing patience. Her eyes were repeatedly drawn to the opening of his shirt, but more worryingly was the niggling thought that if he didn't take her to bed, then she truly had no idea what he was after. That thought was too unfamiliar… and too worrying. Adelma had never been afraid of the unknown, but this was one unknown she really didn't want to explore.

Radish returned with the latest round of rums, and Adelma grabbed hers, downed it, and slammed it back down.

"So you gonna take me home or what?" There. Now things could return to more familiar territory. If he said yes, they would leave. If he said no, she could get offended and pick a fight. And the thought of a fight was growing ever more appealing.

Radish quirked an eyebrow. "Just like that?"

"Well yeah, just like that. What was you expecting— poetry and ballads?"

Radish looked immensely amused, which only annoyed Adelma further.

"Anyone tell you you're as irritating as you are big?"

"Never having just propositioned me, no." Radish's smiled widened.

"First time for everything, and all. So?" Adelma's patience was fraying to its last threads. She felt like she was on the edge of a cliff, leaning forward and about to fall at any moment. If Radish didn't take her home right now, she would punch him. In fact, maybe she would punch him irrespective.

"Reckon I might want to take you home, yeah." Radish's eyes twinkled.

Adelma snorted, feeling relieved. *There, back on firm ground.* She stood up. "Well why didn't you say that right away instead of wasting time talking to me all night?"

"Maybe I was just enjoying your company. Anyway, you seemed to be having fun, too." Radish stood up.

"That ain't no reason for anything," Adelma replied crossly, feeling once again like she was on the edge of something, something unfamiliar and daunting. "So hurry up. I got stuff to do tomorrow, and I wanna be up early."

Radish winked. "Don't worry. I'll have you satisfied and asleep in no time."

That was better. Just the kind of nonsense bravado she was used to. She would leave his place as soon as they were done and never see him again.

CHAPTER 8

Adelma awoke slowly in the morning light, feeling surprisingly groggy and disoriented. Grumbling, she stretched then jumped with fright as the sheet moved next to her and an arm extended itself across her stomach. She jumped out of bed, crashed into a bedside table that hadn't existed until that very moment, and fell down with it in a loud crash.

A man sat up, pushing the sheet aside. "That's an interesting way to get out of bed," Radish said. "Is that how you get up every morning?"

"What the hell you doing in my house?" Adelma growled.

Radish looked around. "I'm pretty sure this is my house. But I'm not much of a morning person, so I could be wrong."

Adelma look at the bedside table. She didn't have a bedside table. She also took in the room. Neat, simple, and most definitely not hers.

"Why am I in your room?" she snarled.

Radish frowned, looking genuinely concerned. "You suggested I take you home last night, remember?"

"Yeah, but I…" *I was supposed to leave the moment we were done.*

Radish's concern faded back into a smile. "You fell asleep pretty quickly."

Adelma stood up, not wanting to keep talking while on the floor. "Anyway, what was that all about, putting your arm across me like that? You didn't half give me a fright."

"I think people call it cuddling," Radish told her. "Although I don't think we got far enough for it to qualify."

Adelma spluttered. "Seriously? Cuddling? What are you? A two-year-old?"

"If I am, I'm a pretty big toddler. Precocious boy." Radish's grin widened.

"Stop smiling." Adelma scowled, still profoundly unsettled.

"Come on, you have to admit it's pretty funny."

"That you go around cuddling people? It ain't funny. It's disturbing. Ain't you embarrassed?"

Radish lay back against his pillow. "I ain't never embarrassed. Waste of time, if you ask me."

Adelma agreed with that, but she wasn't about to tell him. "Where are my clothes?" she grumbled instead.

"Near the front door, from what I remember." Radish winked.

"Damn your eyes! Stop smiling at me." Adelma stalked out of the bedroom into a nicely furnished sitting room decorated with items that clearly weren't from Damsport.

She guessed it was a collection of memorabilia from places Radish had visited in his travels. Places Adelma could only guess at, and she felt a longing to discover them for herself.

Strewn across the floor were her clothes, most of them by the door, as Radish had said. She yanked them on angrily, moving as fast as she could.

Radish had put on a pair of trousers, and he came out into the sitting room, yawning and stretching. He looked as impressive without a shirt on as she'd guessed back in the pub. The sight of him brought back a flash from the previous night, but Adelma shoved it away quickly.

She frowned. "I'm busy. I got stuff to do today. You're wasting my time with all this sleeping so damned late."

"I wasn't aware I was the one making you sleep. But please, don't let me keep you." Radish opened the door and stood aside. "Good luck today."

Still feeling profoundly disturbed by the whole encounter, Adelma stalked past him quickly and left without saying goodbye. The sooner she could forget about the whole thing, the better.

***

Once things were a little clearer in her mind, Adelma went over the previous night's events. *Not* the night with Radish, though. Rather, the fantastic titbit that had fallen in her lap about Teraverre and opium. That needed further investigation.

Still feeling uncharacteristically frazzled, Adelma decided to buy the best maps she could find for Teraverre and the surrounding areas, sparing no expense. If she was going to set up a smuggling route no one had yet done, she couldn't afford to cut corners. Smugglers like Radish knew their business, after all.

She scowled with annoyance at being reminded of him again, and shook herself. She had put aside a little money to act as a buffer against days when the fishing might be poor. Buying the maps reduced her buffer to an uncomfortable level, though, so she'd have to be careful. If she had too many bad fishing days in a row, she would be skirting dangerously close to being as broke as a dock rat.

With that in mind, she made careful sacrifices, ordering watered-down beer at the Arms and no rum, like she'd done towards the end of her Da's life.

"Don't look so pleased," she grumbled at Kriss, who handed her the beer.

"I just think it'll do you good to be off the sauce for a few days."

"Do me good, do me good," Adelma muttered.

She sipped the cat's piss—weak cat's piss at that. At least her head would be clear as lagoon waters. How could a person be fun and full of life when drinking something as inspiring as a limp handshake? Whereas a thick, strong ale, downed with a shot rum—that warmth in the belly and that energy in the blood made a person feel like they could conquer the world. Adelma looked up longingly at the bar counter.

Kriss raised an eyebrow at her. "You can't afford it, remember?"

Adelma nodded. *Business first.* She looked back down at her maps. Following the island's coast with her fingers, she muttered to herself, "Teraverre."

She'd been poring over the maps for a while when someone came to stand next to her. "Anyone told you that you look like the wrong end of a badger's arse?" the man asked. He was bearing a wide grin, and Adelma recognised the insult for what it was: an invitation for a fight. The Old Girl's Arms was a brawling pub, where people went when in the mood for a scrap. It was early, so the pub was still quiet.

"Give me an hour," she replied. "I need to do some work here, and then I'm all yours."

"Sure, catch you later."

Moments later, he was fighting with someone else. The sound of them rolling around on the ground was comforting as Adelma continued to stare at the maps, trying to figure a way into Teraverre.

After an hour, she had to admit Radish had been right. It seemed there really was no way to get into Teraverre without passing through the customs funnel. Teraverre was surrounded by a system of thick iron defence chains that would make it impossible for a ship to pass through without getting wrecked. They formed a perimeter around the island, the ends hammered into rocks that jutted out of the water. There would be chains just beneath the water, probably rocks, too. Attempting to sail into that would be suicide.

Adelma slid her finger over the funnel-shaped entrance that faced south. *Teraverri customs.* She sipped the watery brew and grimaced. *Gods, it's weaker than straw tossed on a storm's wind.*

She tapped the Teraverri customs. If the only way into the island was through customs, she either had to find a way to hide the goods so they were impossible to find, or ensure she didn't get searched.

She downed the rest of the cat's piss. "Hey, Kriss, store these in a safe place for me, would you?" She rolled up the maps and handed them over. Adelma grinned. "I feel a fight coming on."

With a joyful bellow, she threw herself into the rapidly growing melee in the middle of the pub, kicking up the sawdust into a happy mess.

***

The following day, after going out to fish and selling the day's catch, Adelma decided to go see Mercy. They were old friends, and as crackpot as Mercy was, she truly was the best source of information Adelma knew of. Short of the library, probably, if you were the type disposed to spend time with your nose in books, which Adelma wasn't.

Adelma had met Mercy when they were kids, shortly after learning to fight the bullies away. Fresh from her victories, Adelma had come across Mercy being tormented by other older kids. Mercy had been a small, sickly, and extremely weird child. Adelma had produced the brass knuckles again, and that had been the end of that. Not many seven-year-olds carried knuckle dusters in their pockets, after all.

Somehow, in spite of having absolutely nothing in common, Mercy and Adelma had gradually become friends—or as close to friends as Mercy could get. As Adelma had built her reputation as someone not to be messed with, she'd extended it over Mercy, like pulling a blanket over a small child. People gave the little weirdo as wide a berth as they did Adelma. These days, it made little difference—Mercy had grown into a recluse who rarely left the house.

Adelma knocked at the door. "Mercy, it's me!"

Silence. After a moment, a faint rustle indicated that Mercy had checked her peephole.

"Mercy, open up. You know it's me. You seen me and heard my voice."

Still nothing.

"Burn my body, you bloody stubborn woman. Let me *in*!"

"You know you've got to use the secret knock, so why don't you just *do* it?" Mercy replied from behind the door.

"Because you seen and heard me! You're talking to me. You *know* it's me."

"What if you've got someone holding you hostage?"

Adelma threw her hands up to the sky, shaking her head in disbelief. "You just *seen* me. You can see there ain't no one here with me. And if I was being kept hostage, then you just told them about the secret knock."

Silence.

Adelma grumbled. There was no winning an argument with a locked door. She went through the complicated motions of the secret knock that said all was fine. There was another secret knock that signified she was in distress.

And a third one, but Adelma couldn't remember that one or what it was for—not that she'd ever needed to use it.

Finally, after much clunking, the door opened, revealing only gloom. Adelma quickly entered, and Mercy laboriously went through all of the solid steel locks that kept the door safe. Adelma had made the mistake of pointing out that she would be able to hack the door down with her axes, so Mercy had reinforced it with steel bars.

"Can't be too careful," Mercy said reproachfully once she was done. "You should know that by now."

Adelma followed her down the short hallway. Mercy's parents had passed quite a long time ago, but they'd had plenty of time to initiate their daughter into their weird world of hoarding and conspiracy theories.

Entering her house was like stepping into some otherworldly warren. Every surface was covered with piles of newspapers—Mercy hadn't thrown away any of the thousands hoarded by her parents. Adelma knew from experience that the kitchen was stocked well enough to allow Mercy to survive for several years on canned and dry food, and she had her own water tank in the basement.

Mercy was pretty well-off, although no one could tell, given that she lived like a rat in a cave. Adelma had given up trying to understand any of it, settling instead for acceptance. She barely noticed the piles of odd, broken objects, which seemed to have been salvaged from people's rubbish, dotted all over the room.

As usual, the shutters were closed, letting in only narrow strips of light through the gaps between their slats. The lack of light and fresh air made the place smell as old and musty as a tomb.

"I'm so sorry 'bout your old man," Mercy said, looking at the wall slightly to Adelma's left. Her glasses were thick as the bottom of a rum bottle. She blinked, her eyes magnified by her lenses. "They got to him in the end." She shook her head sadly. "I told you—I told you to put a padlock on your food. Can't never be too careful."

She took one of the two chairs in the sitting room and gestured for Adelma to take the other. A canister containing Mercy's tea had a combination padlock to it, as did the opening to the hot water kettle. This was to ward off any poisoning attempts, apparently.

Mercy picked up a notebook and flicked through the pages. "The date of his death matches with the Kushanian's biggest market day. If we take into consideration the patterns of the fish schools and the number of stalls currently active in the Great Bazaar, do you know what we get? Hmm?"

Adelma removed a pile of broken things from her chair.

"Careful!" Mercy stood up and rushed over to carefully check over the items—a comb missing most of its teeth, a knot of old hair, a cracked plate, and the torso and legs of a doll.

Adelma sat down. "My Da drank himself to death, Mercy. I know it—we all know it. Ain't some conspiracy from Kushania or no one else."

"That's what *they* want you to think." Mercy pushed her glasses back on her nose once her inspection was done. She was still a small thing, all tiny, fragile bones. Her hair frizzed in an unkempt halo around her head, and her brown skin still had the same unhealthy pallor she'd had as a child. "You shouldn't dismiss it so casually. Because one of the Widow's gambling dens in Bayog flooded last night."

Adelma kept silent, knowing what was coming next.

"If you look at the report from the Enclosed Docks," Mercy continued, "the flood coincides with the departure of a tinned sardine merchant. Do you see? If we add the number of people who passed through Seam Street on that day—" Mercy headed to the wall and began to scribble feverishly on one of the diagrams pasted on the walls. "Adelma, I think I could blow this thing *wide open*."

"I ain't got no doubt about that."

"If *they* don't get to me first," Mercy replied darkly. "I really wonder what your Da knew. Must have been something big. Dammit, I should have done an interview with him at the end."

Any time Mercy's theories didn't pan out, it was because *they* had somehow managed to get one step ahead of her. Adelma had never received a straight answer about who this mysterious "they" were, and it was another thing she'd given up on trying to understand.

"I'm in need of some information, Mercy," she said, changing the subject. She had no desire to discuss her father's death or Mercy's latest crackpot theory about it.

"Ah-ha. Very good—what do you need?"

"Nothing in Damsport. What can you tell me about Teraverre?" Adelma explained about Assurak and her plan to impress the Widow by smuggling opium onto the island. "No one has ever done it before, and I wanna be the first. Ain't no one gonna turn me away if I can pull something like that off. And then Assurak can go piss up a mast." Adelma grinned at the idea. Damn but it would be good to see the look on his face when she returned victorious.

Mercy squinted at her. "That's a solid plan, given what I understand about the Widow. But as to Teraverre, I can't tell you much. My sources don't bring me much international news, and I tend to focus more on the local events."

Adelma grimaced. "I was worried you might say that." The library would be her best bet, then. The place was full of books with more information than a person could need. The problem was that when she tried to read, letters tended to jump and swap places, making deciphering words a real bugger.

And it was one of the few things that all her strength was completely useless to fix. She couldn't intimidate the problem, either. Nor could she argue with it.

"I'll come with you and take out the books we need on my library account," Mercy said.

"Nah, don't be silly. I'll be fine."

"You don't have a library account."

Adelma shrugged. "I'll make do without one."

"Librarians don't mess around. You won't get any books without an account."

"Fine," Adelma sighed. "So I'll open an account or whatever. It's fine, anyway. I were just hoping you'd have something in all them ledgers of yours. But you know, if you don't, it's really no big deal."

"Adelma, you need to fill in a form to open an account," Mercy said gently.

"So?" Adelma glared at Mercy. "It's *fine.*"

Mercy gave a small smile. "You're right. It's fine. I just figured you'd jump at the opportunity to get me out of the house, that's all."

Adelma was startled. She'd not thought of that. "Oh, well…"

"But no, it's fine. I'll let you get on and stay here." Mercy wrinkled her nose. "I don't want to go outside anyway."

"Hold on, now. It would do you a world of good to get outside. Get some sun on you. The rate you're going, one day, I'll mistake you for a northern milkskin."

"I don't want to go out."

"Mercy, you need to get outside. A walk would do you good, too. You need exercise. I mean, look at you! I bet I could snap your leg in half. You need muscle. You need *sun.* Actually what you really need is some time out at sea on my boat—"

"Alright, alright, I'll come to the library," Mercy said hurriedly, looking worried at the mention of Adelma's boat. "Give me a minute to get ready."

It wasn't until Mercy was unlocking her front door that Adelma realised Mercy had manipulated her expertly. *The little bugger.*

Mercy squinted and cringed away from sunlight as she opened her front door, even though she had on tinted optics. She took a careful, grudging step out, with all the wariness of a woman about to stick her hands in a basket full of crabs.

"Come on, Mercy," Adelma coaxed. It would have been months since her friend had last been out.

"You owe me extra for this," Mercy muttered. "Padlocks on your food. Deal?"

Adelma rolled her eyes to the sky. "Deal," she muttered.

"I'll check in person," Mercy added.

Adelma smiled at that. "A second trip out? Sounds like a plan."

Mercy muttered darkly at that, adding a few curses, before she began locking her door, her movements awkward. She'd loaded herself up with weapons, but had been so paranoid about camouflaging them that she'd be incapable of drawing any of them with any kind of speed. Not that she was in any shape to fight anyway.

As they headed out, Mercy's fear became palpable. She put Adelma in mind of a hermit crab that had stepped out of its shell, its soft body exposed and vulnerable to potential predators. She gave off such a strong prey signal that she would have been catching the attention of every criminal in the near vicinity.

"D'you want me to keep my hand on your shoulder?" Adelma asked gently.

Mercy gave a jerky nod. They'd come up with this system years ago, as Mercy had become more and more afraid of the outside. Adelma put her left hand on Mercy's shoulder in a clear show of ownership. She kept her right hand hovering by her right battle axe.

There was really no need for the show of bravado—it had been a long time since anyone had attacked Adelma in the street, and there was no reason that would change today. But this way, people weren't even likely to risk approaching her for a chat, which would be best. Anyone coming near right now was likely to frighten the crap out of Mercy.

Mercy began to trot towards the library, head jerking left and right as she scanned the streets for danger.

***

Adelma had never seen the point of books, unless it was to prop something up—and even then, they were far from the best tool for the job. Bricks were better, and they could break a window, too.

Libraries were therefore a rather mystifying concept. She understood the advantage of having lots of information stored in one place, but the confusing thing was the weirdoes who seemed to think spending a day in there was enjoyable. It really took all sorts to make a world.

The Damsian library was housed in a tall tower that stuck out of the area surrounding it like a finger pointing at the sky. Adelma chuckled to herself as she wondered if it was flipping the rest of the city off. That, at least, she could get behind. It made the library feel more like her kind of place.

The building was only a year or so old. Before, it had been a regular place, but apparently, the Head Machinist had decided that Damsport needed a modern library. Apparently it was considered a marvel of modern engineering, or some such nonsense. The building of the library had actually delayed the completion of the cranes on the Enclosed Docks, the ones that unloaded heavy cargo. Lunacy. That was far more valuable than some fancy getup to store books. Why did books need technology anyway? Surely you just had to stack them in a pile, and that was job done.

Adelma and Mercy reached the library, and they entered to find themselves in a small, dark room furnished with a single desk. Behind it sat a tiny woman with a pinched face. She looked Adelma over, clearly disapproving.

"I'll be making a number of borrows today," Mercy announced, trotting past the woman.

Adelma could feel Mercy's shoulder relaxing now that they were indoors again. She muttered a curse under her breath at the idiots who'd beaten Mercy up as a child.

Adelma felt sure that if no one had bothered Mercy back then, she wouldn't have turned into such a recluse.

They stepped through a door and into the library proper. They stood at the edge of the tower part of the library, and she looked all the way up to the glass dome that let sunlight pour in. Each level of the library hugged the wall, leaving a circular opening in the centre of the tower. In the middle, a corkscrew staircase coiled all the way up to the top floor. The staircase was copper, so clean and polished, it gleamed. It was connected with each of the library floors by narrow walkways, along which small mechanical creatures scuttled, carrying books on their backs.

"You go sit at that desk there," Mercy whispered, pointing at a bank of desks topped with green leather. She headed over to a large, complicated-looking machine.

Adelma went to sit at one of the desks. She eased herself onto a chair that looked like it might collapse beneath her. It held, luckily.

She frowned her disapproval at the lampshade made of a hollowed out, curved turtle shell. Animals of the sea should remain in the sea, unless they were to be eaten, and even then, their remains should be returned to the sea. She wasn't sure that particular turtle had been eaten. Maybe she'd have a word with the librarian later. Lecture her on leaving turtles alone.

Adelma was startled out of her thoughts by something metallic thumping against her leg. One of the automatons had appeared, bearing a book.

"Excellent." Adelma smiled and reached down for the book.

"Shhh," a man next to her said.

Adelma turned to glower at him, and he glared back, completely unafraid despite his diminutive size. Impressed, she gave him a nod in acknowledgement and respect. It was rare to find non-criminals who were able to face her without fear, especially if the person in question was half her size. It seemed that book weirdoes had a good reserve of bravery when it came to protecting their sacrosanct library silence. *Who knew?*

Mercy was still hard at work at the large machine, and more and more automatons appeared, each bearing books. By the time Mercy was done, there was an impressive stack on the desk. Adelma managed to decipher the word Teraverre on one, but luckily, Mercy came over and inspected the books.

"Good, all there. Let's go. Home. Now."

***

They left the library, Adelma cradling the books in one hand, the other hand back on Mercy's shoulder. "Thanks, Mercy. Can't tell you how much of a help this is."

"You can thank me when I'm safely back home," Mercy said tightly.

"Sure thing. And I'll help you with them books, too," Adelma said dubiously, looking at the large stack. It was a lot of information, to be sure, and that was good, but it would mean a lot of reading.

"Don't be ridiculous. You'd be worse than useless. Leave it with me, and I'll send word when I have something useful. Now, faster."

Mercy's trotting increased in speed, but her legs were so short, Adelma kept up easily at a slightly fast walk.

"As I live and breathe, Mercy? Is that you?" a man said, coming towards them.

"Radish, now is *not* the time," Mercy snapped without slowing her trot.

Adelma's stomach sank. *Radish? Why him, of all the people in Damsport to cross paths with?* She felt an uncomfortable heat rise up her throat at the memory of the night they'd spent together and worse, the morning.

Radish fell into step with them. "I'm just shocked to see you out and about, Mercy."

Adelma frowned, as something else occurred to her— and it was a relief to have an interruption to her previous thoughts. She looked from Mercy to Radish. "You two know each other?"

"Radish is one of my regular information providers."

Mercy traded information with a number of people in order to feed her crackpot theories.

Radish gave Adelma an impressed glance. "I've never managed to get Mercy out of the house before."

"Only one reason Mercy would brave the outside." Adelma jerked her chin down towards the books.

Radish nodded at once. "Of course—information."

"I'm so glad you're both enjoying this delightful conversation while my safety is at risk," Mercy said, "but can you please wait until I'm home? Radish, you can escort the both of us back—someone might try to mug us for the books. Two escorts will be better than one."

"Of course."

"And then, Adelma, you can ask Radish about Teraverre, too. See if he can provide us with a rough idea of which direction to look."

Adelma winced as Mercy dropped the word *Teraverre* so casually. She didn't want anyone knowing her plans—least of all another smuggler. And she also *really* didn't want to be talking to Radish again.

"Teraverre?" Radish raised an eyebrow.

Adelma grunted.

"Radish can be trusted," Mercy snapped. "And I need some direction in my research. Otherwise, it'll be like looking for a needle in a haystack and take twice as long. Oh! Stone the gulls, we're almost back."

Mercy's trot increased until it was very nearly a run, and they soon reached her door.

"I think it's best that just you and me work on this," Adelma told Mercy as the small woman started the laborious process of unlocking the door.

"Nonsense. This is the most efficient way."

Adelma shook her head, not meeting Radish's eye. It didn't help that he had begun to grin broadly.

"Adelma," Mercy snapped, her voice making it clear that she was close to her breaking point. The door opened at that moment, and she turned and snatched several books from Adelma, throwing them through the doorway. "If I can brave the outdoors, then you can trust another person." She grabbed the rest of the books. "Now go talk to Radish and report back when you got something of interest." Mercy rushed inside, slammed the door shut, and clunking sounds rang out as she pulled the locks into place.

Adelma glared at the door for a moment, feeling her frustration grow. Radish, damn his eyes, had failed to get the hint and disappear. She couldn't quite work out what was worse—that Mercy had alerted another smuggler to her plans or to be seeing Radish so soon after…

Best not to think about that.

Still, she'd been so sure it would be easy to avoid seeing him for a long time. She couldn't make a big deal about it, though, or he would guess she wanted to avoid him. What she needed was to project supreme indifference.

The wide grin on Radish's face made it clear that he was far from indifferent. Adelma suddenly wanted to punch him.

"Why d'you look so damned pleased?" she grumbled. "And why the hell do people insist on lumping you with me?"

"They probably have a lot more sense than you do. Now, I'm not opposed to giving you information about Teraverre, but it will cost you. A drink at least. In fact, make that several drinks. Hand and Tankard?"

With an irritated sigh, Adelma threw her hands up in the air and then stomped off. "Hurry up," she called over her shoulder. "Let's get this over and done with as quickly as possible."

She would have been incapable of naming the feeling that was roiling in her stomach, but she didn't like it. The feeling was foreign, it was uncomfortable, and the sooner this was all done and forgotten about, the better.

93

CHAPTER

10

"So why d'you want to know about Teraverre?" Radish asked once they were settled at a table in the Hand and Tankard.

"Because."

Radish looked amused. "Well, I suppose the deal is for me to do the talking, so fair enough." He turned serious. "I know that just because no one's smuggled opium into Teraverre before doesn't mean it's impossible. Eventually, someone will figure out how to get it done. But it's a dangerous game to play." His eyes were full of concern.

Adelma frowned in reply, annoyed that he felt the need to be worried about her. "The deal was for information, not for you sticking your nose into my business where it don't belong. I know my business. I know what I'm about, and I definitely don't need you to look after me."

"You're right—we've been over that before, haven't we?" Radish gave a wry smile, and Adelma realised he was referring to that very first time they'd met, back when she'd decked Assurak. "I just wouldn't want you to get yourself into a bad situation, that's all."

"Why do you care anyway? Makes no odds to you if I get into a spot of trouble, so why bother?"

Radish leaned back in his seat. "That's a good question. I guess the answer is that I get to choose what I bother about. Believe it or not, Adelma, I like you. You're different. I saw the way you were with Mercy just now, and I heard about you caring for your Da at the end…"

Adelma looked down at her hands, a weird lump forming in her throat.

"Thing is," Radish continued. "I think beneath it all, you're quite a gentle soul. Although I reckon it would take a serious amount of patience or stubbornness, and strength, to be able to get to that. Luckily, I enjoy challenges." Radish grinned broadly. "That, and nice girls bore me…"

Again, Adelma would have been incapable of naming all the odd, unfamiliar feelings in the pit of her stomach. She began to worry she'd eaten something bad. Maybe she would throw up shortly. *Better out than in.*

But in the meantime, she wanted the conversation to move—and quickly, because she really didn't want to be discussing her Da now, of all times. She cleared her throat, trying to dislodge the lump that had formed there. "Alright, enough of this nonsense. We made a deal for information, so get on with it and tell me about Teraverre."

"You're right," Radish said easily. Did the man ever get ruffled by anything? "You asked for information, so here goes."

He began to recount the few trips he'd taken to Teraverre. He hadn't been there much, on account that he didn't do business there, but he had a good way with story, and he painted a vivid picture.

"And streets so clean, I swear you could eat off the cobblestones. I mean, I guess it's nice and all, having clean streets, but the Teraverri are pretty anal about it all. Makes it feel like the place ain't quite real, you know? I think a city needs a bit of filth, a bit of grit."

Adelma heartily agreed with that.

"And they're real paranoid, too," Radish continued. "Be careful that you don't ever go with the slightest symptom like a cough or a runny nose. We were supposed to go visit, not for a job. One of the men on my crew had a cold. Alright, maybe it was influenza, but it weren't nothing life-threatening. Those paranoid bastards wouldn't hear a word of it. Stuck us straight in quarantine. I mean, as far as quarantine docks go, it's pretty damn decent, same as everything they do. Clean, fresh food daily, and they even supply medicine. My sailor recovered, but they still refused to let us in and just booted us back out to sea." Radish shook his head.

"Why did they let you stay in quarantine if they had no intention of letting you into the city?"

"Partly because of this agreement between countries that if a ship is in need of assistance, they will be given access to the quarantine docks. They obviously decided we needed assistance. But also because if a ship really is in a bad way and they turn it away, the sailors might be desperate enough to try and swim to shore, which would then bring the sickness in anyway. The quarantine docks mean they could keep an eye on us. You wouldn't believe the number of coastal guards patrolling our side of the island."

Adelma nodded, taking it all in. Radish hadn't told her about the quarantine dock with any intention other than to share a story and have a bit of a grumble—that much was clear. But it had given her an idea, not that she would let him know that. She remembered Lukas not being allowed to dock in Damsport. A ship that was clearly carrying disease might not be searched as thoroughly at customs, if it just wanted to use the quarantine dock… and getting the opium from the quarantine dock to the shore would be easier than getting it past the customs officers.

Adelma felt a shiver of excitement. That was definitely something she could work with. Not wanting to betray what she was thinking, she moved the conversation on quickly. Best to lull Radish into a false sense of security with more general banter. He didn't seem to mind, and they ordered another round of drinks, trading stories and jokes and generally having a nice time. Adelma felt herself relaxing, the odd tension in her stomach dissipating. She lost herself in the easy flow of conversation Radish seemed so good at creating.

It wasn't until they were heading back to Radish's house that Adelma wondered if she'd truly been the one to distract Radish and not the other way around. Maybe it was all the beer she'd drunk, but she found she didn't really care.

***

This time, when Adelma woke up, she didn't fall out of the bed or crash into anything. While she wouldn't go as far as to say that the sight of Radish's bedroom was now familiar, at least it wasn't completely disorientating.

The clean, whitewashed walls. The dark-stained wooden beams, treated to protect them against rot, insects, and humidity. The slightly faded furniture made from good wood. The sheets that smelt like soap.

"Good morning," Radish said, stirring next to her.

Adelma suddenly felt so awkward, she froze rigid.

"Well, I'm glad to see that you're not crashing into the furniture this time." Radish gave her a sleepy smile.

Adelma's awkwardness disappeared as quick as a fart on the wind, giving way to anger. She jumped out of bed. "Let's get something very clear. This ain't happening again, got it?"

"What's not happening again?"

"Last night. This whole ridiculous situation. Wipe that smile off your face. I don't know what you think is going on here, but I got work to do. I'd have left in the middle of the night, but for some reason, I fell asleep. Again."

When Radish grinned, Adelma's scowl deepened. It was amazing just how often she wanted to punch something when around him. "Don't look at me like that! I'm tired, is all. Lots on my mind of late. But that don't mean it's a reason to get into any kind of sentimental rubbish."

"Sentimental rubbish? I said good morning and congratulated you for not breaking my bedside table."

"Exactly, and that's quite enough." Adelma knew she wasn't making much sense, but she didn't care. "I'm getting dressed, I'm going my way, and you can get on with your day. Got it?"

Radish turned serious and nodded, although she could see the edges of the smile tugging at the corners of his lips.

"I said don't look at me like that!" she snapped.

At that, Radish grinned. "I meant what I said last night, you know. I like you. I think you're great."

Adelma was so startled, she somehow managed to inhale her own saliva. She spluttered and coughed, staggering sideways into the bedside table. "Damn that table!" she yelled.

Radish frowned. "I already told you that I liked you last night, so it shouldn't be that much of a shock, surely?"

He might have done, but it was feeling much more uncomfortably real in the morning light. Adelma angrily yanked her clothes on without replying. Once she was dressed, she stormed out without bothering to say goodbye. That was her done with *that*. This time, she wouldn't see Radish again—she had all the information she needed and therefore no more need of him. And what a relief that was.

The early light was tinged with pink, and she marched off quickly, heading back towards her own house. The walk did her good, loosening her body.

She yawned and then yawned again. She hadn't lied about being tired. In a moment of utterly ridiculous stupidity, she briefly—*very* briefly—thought that maybe it would have been nice not to have stormed out of Radish's place quite so quickly. His room was comfortable and pleasant to be in, after all.

Adelma scoffed at herself, pushed the thought away, and rolled her eyes. Clearly, Radish's idiocy was contagious.

Speaking of contagion, I best go see Mercy to tell her about Teraverri quarantine.

Adelma stalked off to get on with her day. Serious work and lots to do. For some reason, though, she kept smiling. To remedy that, she made a point of scowling at every person who crossed her path.

Two days later, Adelma spent another night with Radish. A complete accident. She needed a little more information from him—at Mercy's request, of course. And she'd decided that if she made a big deal of avoiding him, then that wasn't being indifferent. Whereas, if she didn't mind running into him…which seemed to be happening surprisingly often, if she stopped to think of it.

Over the next couple of weeks, Adelma settled into a surprisingly comfortable routine. She spent her days fishing, earning the money she needed to live. As soon as that was done, she went straight to Mercy's to check on progress in researching the Teraverri quarantine docks.

Mercy had had the right of it. Looking through those books full of small type and complicated words would have taken Adelma months. She didn't have that kind of patience. The books would have been torn up in a fit of frustrated rage by now. Better to leave Mercy to it.

And Mercy had delivered as only Mercy could. They'd picked up more books from the library, along with ledgers and records from the Damsian docks. Mercy made a list of symptoms and behaviours that would cause the customs officer to send a ship straight to quarantine without a search for fear of contagion. Those ships, of course, were never allowed to shore even after recovering and were escorted out as soon as they were fit to sail again. Mercy also found out what items Teraverre imported most frequently—the kind of cargo customs officers would be accustomed to finding aboard arriving ships.

All the information was fuel to Adelma's fire, and she slowly figured how she might use the quarantine dock to deliver the opium. The bones of her plan were simple: if she could use a version of her lobster pot with their delayed floaters to hold the opium in secret under the water for a few weeks, she could then arrange to have the pot collected around the time the floater rose up to the surface, and then get it delivered.

Keeping the floater underwater for as long as a couple of weeks was proving tricky, though. The arborum paste didn't last long enough, no matter how much of the stuff she used. She'd have to figure something else out.

It was a simple plan, but she felt confident that it was sound. She was fully aware that she was risking her life to get opium into Teraverre, but that didn't truly bother her. Failure wasn't something she considered a realistic possibility.

Once she had ironed out the finer details, she'd go to the Widow. And once she'd pulled the whole thing off, Adelma would be set, and Assurak would get what he deserved.

The key, however, was to approach the Widow at the right time: late enough that Adelma had time to make sure her setup was watertight, but before any real investment or risk on her part. She had no problem taking risks, but only if she was guaranteed a good payout.

After each session with Mercy, Adelma headed to the Old Girl's Arms for a drink and to mull over whatever they'd discussed. More often than not, Radish showed up during the evening. At first, Adelma found it irritating, mostly because it was hard to think with him in the pub, even when he wasn't talking to her. But she gradually found herself looking forward to his arrival.

Adelma would never have admitted it, but on the nights he didn't show up, she felt disappointed. She even once got close to going to look for him, but pride and sense won out. She wasn't ever going to be the kind of woman to trail after some man like a heartsick little milksop.

More often than not, when she did see Radish, she ended up spending the night at his place. Mornings were growing a little less awkward, although she still felt the need to hurry away quickly. Radish was too comfortable. Too happy to have her there. Too…everything was wrong really, in the mornings. At night, though, with the help of beer, things were easier.

She also eventually found a machinist who could engineer a solution for her adapted lobster pot. A watertight weighted container would be made to contain the opium, so it would sink to the bottom once dropped in the sea. The machinist would also put together a box to contain the floater and its slender rope.

The box could be set to open using a delayed clockwork mechanism, also enclosed in a watertight compartment. The little cogs would turn slowly and continuously for two weeks, after which time they would stop, and the box would open, releasing the floater. As with the lobster pot, the floater's slender string would be tied to a sturdy rope. Whoever she organised for the pick up could catch the floater and use it to bring up the thick cord, which would then be used to haul up the container.

The mechanism would even have a special combination of switches that would have to be flicked in the right order for it to be set off. A perfect solution.

The cost of all this, however, was quite a bit more than Adelma had expected. Something to bear in mind during her negotiations with the Widow, when the time was right.

Eventually, Adelma's preparations had gone as far as they could without her going to Teraverre in person to scope things out. She thought long and hard about whether to contact the Widow before leaving, but she decided to do the trip first, even though it would be quite an expense.

If the Widow smelt the slightest weakness or uncertainty, she might not believe Adelma capable of pulling it off. Adelma had to *know* in her bones that the plan would work, and for that she would need to go see Teraverre for herself.

It took her a couple more weeks of working hard and scrimping all the money she could to prepare. She continued to see Radish during that time, who in spite of having no ship and no work, still seemed unbothered by the situation. He either had a decent chunk of money tucked away or some other income Adelma didn't know about. Either way, he was in no hurry to finally decide whether he was giving up life as a smuggler.

Best of all, though, he seemed to have completely bought her pretence of having lost interest in Teraverre. It had occurred to her that she might need a partner in the venture, but she'd cross that bridge when she came to it. *When it comes down to it, you can only trust yourself, my girl,* her Da always said. *Best to leave others out of your business.*

The morning of her departure, she woke up at Radish's place. She wasn't sure what was more disturbing: the regularity of how often that occurred or that she wasn't feeling uncomfortable about it anymore. Life had evolved weirdly indeed.

"So how long you gonna be gone?" Radish asked her.

Adelma had made up an excuse for the trip and given him a fake destination. Her plan had to remain *completely* secret. She hadn't even told Kriss about it. The only one who knew was Mercy, and Mercy made an art out of paranoia and secrecy.

"Just over a week, if I don't get any delays." Adelma didn't plan on spending long in Teraverre. She knew exactly what she was looking for once she got there.

"A week, huh?" Radish gave a lopsided grin. He shifted as if he might put an arm around her, and Adelma stiffened at once. Radish gave a rueful shake of his head and settled back into place. "Leaving me alone for a week." He gave a dramatic sigh. "What am I gonna do with my evenings?"

Adelma frowned. "What kind of stupid question's that? You'll do whatever you do when I ain't around." Admittedly, that hadn't been often of late.

"Ah yes, that's right. We take everything literally and with a pragmatic angle."

Adelma frowned. What was wrong with either of those things?

"You'll come look me up when you're back?" Radish asked.

What frightened Adelma most wasn't that Radish had asked the question, it was that she'd almost said yes. Blind panic flared up. *What's happening to me?* And what kind of power did Radish over her?

She climbed out of the bed quickly. "So, what? You're telling me what to do now?" Her nostrils flared. There, anger was better. Soothing, familiar anger. Life was simpler when she was in a fight. It was all the rest that made things complicated.

"Stone the gulls, Adelma, I'm just trying to have a nice chat before you go. And maybe make plans for when you get back. Is that really so bad?"

"It is if you think you can just dictate what I'll be doing."

Radish closed his eyes and pinched his nose. "You know, sometimes you make me feel like it would be more fun to smack my head against a brick wall."

"Well, knock yourself out. Pun intended."

"Is that seriously it? That's really how you're gonna leave today?"

"Reckon it is, yeah. That a problem? That I ain't rolling on my back and saying 'yes, Radish' to everything you say, and—"

"When did I *ever* ask that of you?" Radish thundered so loudly, it startled Adelma into complete silence. His face had darkened like a storm had settled over his features. "Has it occurred to you to appreciate the bloody levels of patience and understanding I've had to deploy to put up with all your nonsense? Has it, for that matter, occurred to you to think of someone other than yourself and your ridiculous principles? Which are bloody dumb, by the way."

"My principles?"

"Yes," Radish snapped, also getting out of bed and getting dressed while Adelma yanked her own clothes on. "Your relentless need to take offence at *everything* that doesn't perfectly match your expectations and to always be so damned secretive—I don't even know where you're really going."

Adelma opened her mouth, but Radish barrelled on. "Don't you dare feed me that piss-poor lie about going to Paladeen."

Adelma's initial shock at seeing Radish so wound up finally faded enough to get angry in turn. "You know what? Ain't nothing dumb about relying on myself, about anticipating that people—like *you*, by the way—are unreliable and eventually will let me down." She pointed an accusing finger at him. "That's smart, that is. And if your precious ego can't handle that, then go piss up a mast!"

Radish let out a joyless laugh. "Ego, seriously? If I had any ego, I wouldn't have been wasting all this time with you."

Adelma was surprised to find that smarted quite a lot. Stung even. Maybe it even hurt. He'd been wasting time with her?

"Ha," she sneered, shoving the hurt way, way down. "You ain't got nothing to do but waste time. You ain't working. You ain't smuggling. What does that make you? At least I've got my plans. At least I'm working towards something. You should count yourself lucky that I spent time with you at all. And you know what? You can go drown in puddle of piss for all I care. I don't ever want to hear from you again."

Adelma slammed the door behind her as she stormed out.

Adelma got her ship ready, her heart still pounding from the argument with Radish. She cursed him repeatedly as she worked, and when a fisherman she knew commented on her foul mood, she gave him a black eye and a loose tooth.

This should have been the start of her first big adventure as a smuggler, and all she could think about was Radish.

"Damn his eyes!" she yelled as she got the sails ready.

His words bounced around her head. He'd been wasting time with her. She was as fun as smacking his head against a brick wall. And he'd wanted her to come look for him once she was back.

"I *said* damn his eyes!" she yelled again. That helped a little.

Finally, she headed out to sea. Sailing never failed to soothe her, and after a couple hours, she found that she was almost calm.

And then the wind died. The sea turned flatter than a flounder's tit, like shimmering blue fabric stretching around her boat. At that, all of Adelma's anger resurfaced, and she yelled curse after insult at the sky, at Radish, at the doctors who'd failed to help her Da, and at her Da for leaving her alone in the first place.

Life had been more straightforward with him around, but right now, no matter how angry she got, she couldn't ignore that she felt hopelessly lost and confused.

She kept busy as best she could until the wind returned, working damn hard not to think of Radish. In all, she lost a day to the bad winds, taking three days to come within sight of the island of Teraverre.

By then, all thoughts of Radish had left her, replaced by the excitement of finally seeing the place she'd been obsessed with for so long.

Teraverre was a volcanic island, rising from the sea in a large peak. The edges were heavily built up. The green vegetation-covered summit rose from the ring of buildings and streets like the tonsured crown of a monk's head.

Out in the water, Adelma could also see the large network of chains that made Terraverre so forbidding to smugglers. The island was surrounded by a smattering of rocky outcrops into which the heavy chains had been nailed. They were all of dark-grey steel, and thick as Adelma's arm.

It made for a startling contrast with the clear water that reached towards the island and the dark green beyond. As she got nearer, Adelma could make out dark shapes in the water, where more chains ran just beneath the surface to wreck any ship tempted to try and make landfall. There was no boat shallow enough to pass without catching on the underwater chains.

The entrance funnel was clearly identifiable, given the massive queue of ships waiting to pass through. Adelma joined the back of the queue. Given the size of it and the slowness of the progression, it was going take her the rest of the day to get past customs.

The checkpoint was large, with several channels through which ships passed, then stopped, as customs officers executed rigorous searches.

As Mercy had explained, they searched everyone, not just the ships carrying cargo. Dogs barked, sent down below-decks to sniff out the presence of opium or other drugs.

Adelma lowered her binoculars, rubbing her arms against the gooseflesh rising on her skin. The air was quite a lot cooler than in Damsport. If Adelma had owned warm clothes, she'd have brought them along. She hadn't the money to spare for new clothes, so instead, she grabbed two jute bags and used them to cover her shoulders. Damsport's heat was definitely preferable.

More ships joined the queue behind her as she waited. The air was heavy with the smoke belched by various steam engines. Adelma wished she had the funds for an engine—moving forward in the queue was awkward with a sailboat. At least the wind was blowing in the right direction. If the wind had been coming straight from the island, it would have been a nightmare.

A postal ship chugged past, going up along the left of the queue. Adelma pulled out her binoculars. The ship approached the checkpoint from the left, entering an unused channel. Several customs officers came to greet it. Paperwork was handed over in some kind of exchange. Adelma wondered if anyone had thought to use a postal ship to smuggle.

She abandoned that idea immediately as she saw two customs officers head below deck. They remained there a good while, no doubt searching through the bags of mail and parcels. Interestingly, though, no dogs were present this side of the checkpoint. The postal ship was eventually allowed into the inner lagoon.

Adelma lowered her binoculars. So there was obviously some kind of priority channel. That was worth remembering—when she was on the opium run and pretending to be carrying disease, she could go straight for this part of the checkpoint, hoisting the flags indicating distress and disease.

The lack of dogs was also an important advantage. If her symptoms were bad enough—and she'd make sure they were—she would be sent to quarantine with only the most cursory of searches. Still, best to make sure the opium would be undetectable by smell.

The queue continued to move slowly. Adelma kept herself busy by observing the quarantine dock and the quarantine station on the shore beyond. Her body tingled. It was one thing to plan in the abstract. It was another to see it all become reality.

Finally, after what seemed like an eternity, Adelma reached the checkpoint.

"Stop!" a Teraverri officer announced, showing the palm of her hand. She held a clipboard under her other arm. Adelma did as she commanded, throwing two coils of rope to the waiting officers. They tethered her ship efficiently.

"Step off the ship, please," the supervising officer said. She had the copper skin and highly prominent cheekbones of a Teraverri, as did the other two officers. All three wore black trousers and black coats.

Adelma complied. The two other officers climbed aboard, along with a dog. They began the most thorough search Adelma had experienced. The dog was everywhere, sniffing planks, rope—everything. Adelma had no doubt that it would be able to smell even a small scrap of opium. She had checked her boat thoroughly to ensure there was absolutely nothing that could be construed as suspicious, but all the same, she found herself growing nervous. Her barrel of freshwater, left above deck to catch any rain, was searched, its inner walls tapped to check for a false bottom. Her food supplies were checked, and the officers pulled apart her nets meticulously.

"I found something," an officer said from below decks.

Adelma's stomach fell into her boots. *Found something? There should have been nothing to find.* She had checked—she'd been so careful. Her mind raced back over the last couple of months. Could she still have opium leftover from the runs she'd made to Airnia?

It seemed to take the officer an age and a half to climb back up above deck. Adelma kept her face neutral, but inside, her mind was whirling. Could she really have been stupid enough to miss something important?

The customs officer climbed out of the boat, onto the checkpoint dock. He held out an earring. Adelma looked at it, in shock. She hadn't spotted it despite all her searching.

"Wedged between two planks," the officer said. "Yours?"

Adelma took the earring and looked it over quickly. The earring was cheap metal, the gold plating scuffed off in places. Even she could tell the gems on it were paste.

Adelma shook her head slowly. "My mother's." Her Da, devastated by losing its mate, had kept the other earring for years.

The supervising officer nodded. She scribbled something on her clipboard. Adelma's throat felt tight. She didn't often think of her mother, mostly because it made her think of her father, which always made her throat squeeze.

One thing was for sure, though, she felt more than a little shaken at the results of the search. She'd known the Teraverri customs officers were thorough, but she hadn't anticipated they would be *that* thorough. She glanced back at the priority channel of the checkpoint, suddenly worried. Very worried. Would she be able to get past and into the quarantine area without being searched?

For the first time in as long as she could remember, Adelma felt doubt. Her plan now seemed as flimsy as tissue paper. Was the risk really worth the payout? Yes, she would become a well-established smuggler, but she would be taking such a huge gamble to get there. There were no other options, though. Assurak had made sure to close off her other paths to smuggling. If she didn't do this, she would be conceding defeat, an absolutely impossible option.

But if she went ahead... *What if...*

"Alright, off you go," the customs officer said.

Adelma readied her boat to sail off, finding herself wishing her Da were still there. He'd have advice. No problem had ever seemed that large when her Da was still alive.

She sailed into Teraverre, feeling a deep loneliness.

CHAPTER

By the time Adelma had reached the Teraverri dock, she'd gotten ahold of herself again. She had a solid plan, and she was here to iron out the last couple of details. All this nonsense, this self-doubt, that wasn't her. A momentary blip.

If, after her inspection here, she felt the plan didn't hold water, then she would toss it aside and figure out something else. If the plan felt reliable to her, that meant it was good. She knew she could rely on her own judgement. Knew it in her bones. Just as her Da had drilled into her.

She'd wanted his advice, but really, she already had it: rely on herself, and only herself, and don't let any wrong against her slip by. That was the crux of his whole life philosophy. So put together a solid plan, become a smuggler for the Widow, and then *crush* Assurak.

Simple.

Adelma paid her docking fee, looking around her in wonder. This was as far removed from the Damsian Enclosed Docks as possible. It was… *nice.*

There was no chaos, no smell. Or rather there *was* a smell—something pleasant, maybe jasmine or some such flower. The people didn't shout or hurry. There were no seedy establishments along the docks, but instead a row of bright places that looked like they had been scrubbed recently. And they were most definitely devoid of drunks stumbling out and prostitutes leading sailors in.

Curious, Adelma entered a drinking hole. Or rather, she reached the entrance and stopped when she saw a placard advertising the beers. The cost had her spluttering and running away. She'd have had to sell a kidney to afford that. And by the looks of Teraverre, there would be no shady back alleys where those kinds of transactions took place.

Luckily, Adelma had come prepared. Mercy had warned her of the exorbitant prices, so Adelma had brought a stash of food and a bottle of rum. She'd sleep in a hammock on her boat, and if all went well, she wouldn't spend a penny of the little money she still had after buying all the supplies for the trip.

Adelma headed off towards where she knew the land quarantine facilities would be. Mercy had dug up some great street maps of Teraverre and copied out the sections Adelma would need—Adelma had only thought to buy nautical maps of the sea around the island.

Just to be safe, she had memorised the routes she would need to take. The last thing she wanted was to stand in the middle of a street with an open map, like some idiot with "mug me" tattooed on her forehead. Although, a city this clean couldn't have cutpurses or muggers more effective than those found in the Rookery—and Adelma could deal with those.

The city of Teraverre was weird. There was no other way to describe it. It just didn't feel... real. The Teraverri patrician was a benevolent dictator who apparently liked things to run in an orderly fashion. Mercy had talked about this at length, and Radish had also mentioned how clean the city was. However, none of it had truly prepared her for the surreal experience of walking through Teraverri streets.

Streets so clean, you could have eaten off the cobblestones. Radish hadn't been embellishing for the sake of a good story. Signs everywhere reminded everyone not to litter. That was odd enough, but people *actually* respected the signs. What kind of city was this where people respected authority? And more importantly, if no one threw anything out in the street, what did the beggars, urchins, and other society dregs live off?

More signs told people not to spit on the floor and that crime wasn't tolerated. One sign even proclaimed that thanks to their patrician's benevolent genius, Teraverre was the only city in the world to be completely free of crime and decadence. Adelma snorted at that. Crime was the most universal human trait, and criminal activity was as old and widespread a profession as prostitution. It would be somewhere in Teraverre, just far out of sight.

Still, though, the average people did seem to live by those rules. Try as she might, she hadn't yet been able to clock a pickpocket or mugger, and the inordinate number of uniformed guards walking about the streets was unsettling.

The shops were all bright, clean, and well organised. Streets were colour-coded, and every building matched. No one, it seemed, stepped out of line. The people were all dressed nicely, or rather there was no obvious poverty. Adelma envied the thicker coats that seemed to be the fashion here—the wind had barely dropped since she'd come ashore, and she was really starting to feel the cold.

Everyone also seemed intensely groomed—shaped eyebrows, dyed hair, and manicured nails, both for men and women. Adelma's nostrils were assaulted by waft after waft of perfume every time she crossed paths with someone—far more unpleasant than getting a sniff of old booze or stale sweat. They also had a real thing for hats— gleaming black top hats rammed atop heads for the men, smaller versions at jaunty angles for the women.

Simply bizarre.

Adelma eventually reached the land quarantine facility. The actual quarantine area was out at sea, as she had seen earlier, but it was linked to the buildings on shore by a pulley system. Small crates of food and basic medical supplies could be winched to the unfortunates stuck in quarantine. The building was nothing to look at—clean like the rest of the city, but plain and ugly. It was deserted at the moment, as she would have expected, given that its workers were only paid when there was a ship in quarantine.

There would only be a couple of workers at most, given that all they did was winch across the supplies and ensure that anything sent back from quarantine was destroyed. Once the quarantined ship had left or everyone had died, two workers would head to the quarantine area, and any rubbish left behind would be incinerated. It was a pretty thorough setup.

Adelma could see the winching system set up on the end of a pier. An incinerator was set up against the quarantine building. Adelma nodded. Mercy truly was a gem. Everything was just as she had described. It was only good sense to verify the information in person, but it seemed like Adelma could simply have shown up with Mercy's explanations, except for one very important detail: she needed someone in Teraverre to help her take the opium to the delivery address.

She walked away from the quarantine area. She didn't believe for a second in the nice, clean facade that the city presented. There was poverty here, as well as corruption and crime. She just needed to find it, and once she was among her kind of people, she could see about hiring someone to work for her.

She turned a corner and came face-to-face with exactly the kind of person she was after. He wasn't anywhere near as ragged as what could be found in Damsport. Still, his clothes were drab and dirty, and he held a broom, sweeping the street.

Two more aspects of the man gave Adelma serious pause. The first was that he wasn't Teraverri. The colour of his skin and his features made him look Damsian—a very auspicious sign. The second was that the man was huge. Larger than her. Larger even than Radish. About the size of her Da. His broom looked like a child's toy in his hands.

"You from Damsport?" Adelma asked him.

The man looked up at her, startled, and then his face broke into a grin. "Ah, you Damsian, too," he said. "Always good to see people from the old country. I miss it, I do, even though I don't remember it much, on account of my Ma and Pa brought me here when I were still titchy. That ain't a figure of speech, mind you. Because when I were small, I were no bigger than a thumb. I grew up fast, is all. Powerful fast grower, me."

Adelma blinked twice, a little taken aback. Then she smiled. "What's your name? I'm Adelma."

"Slothum. But they call me Two Planks, on account of how big I am. Thick as Two Planks, they call me." Two Planks pointed at his massive bicep, grinning.

Adelma bit her lip. "Two Planks?" She felt the familiar anger rising up within her. It was good that Two Planks didn't realise people were having fun at his expense. If that were to happen in front of her, she would gladly make the point that laughing at Two Planks was not good for a person's health, no more than it had been good to mock Mercy.

Despite how big he was, Two Planks didn't have the look of a fighter. He gave out a very slow, calm energy, like a gentle giant—probably why people felt they could get away with insulting him.

"Well, it's nice to meet you, Two Planks. How long you been in Teraverre for?"

Two Planks frowned, looking down at his hands. "I were a little 'un when my Pa brought me over."

Adelma realised he was counting fingers. She also realised that the Teraverri walking past them seemed to be studiously pretending neither of them were there, despite their size and unusual appearances.

"People always ignore you?" she asked him.

Two Planks scratched his head, interrupting his counting. "I guess so. Maybe it's because they don't know my name. Slothum's powerful unusual for a name. My old Ma made it up. I were powerful lazy as a child, see. I slept a lot, like a sloth. And I was no bigger than a thumb—I grew into my size later, so my old Ma said. Anyway, she used to carry me around in her pocket, and it took her a long time to find a name for me, but she called me Slothum."

"Yep, that's an unusual name, for sure," Adelma replied, still looking at the people walking past. An idea was forming in her head. After all, she needed someone who wouldn't draw attention. Two Planks would have seemed like the opposite of that at first sight, but clearly, people treated him like he was invisible, maybe because he was poor, foreign, or both.

That said, Adelma wasn't sure she felt comfortable asking someone who didn't quite have all their marbles to do something dangerous. He might not fully grasp the risks he'd be taking.

"Fifteen," Two Planks said, yanking Adelma out of her thoughts.

She frowned. "What? Fifteen what?"

"Been here fifteen years, now. My old Pa brought us here. Looking to make his fortune, he was. Didn't quite work out. He passed a few years ago, now. My old Ma and I are trying to get back to Damsport, but a place on a ship costs a lot money, and we don't got enough."

Adelma considered. Two Planks's mother might be a better person to talk to. "What would you say if I told you I might have a business opportunity for you what would get you out of Teraverre?"

Two Planks shook his head vigorously. "I ain't going nowhere without my old Ma. Nowhere. No way."

"I meant for you two—you and your Ma to get out of Teraverre. I can make it happen, but I need help with something. Could you take me to your Ma? So I could talk to her?"

Two Planks frowned, considering. "Yeah, I think you better talk to her. I don't know much about business. Leaving Teraverre sure sounds like a good deal, but… yes, you should talk to her. I don't make no decisions without her."

"Alright, good. Well, take me to her."

"Now?" Two Planks looked shocked. "No, no, no. I can't abandon my post. Not before the end of day."

Adelma widened her eyes incredulously. "Post?" She only just managed to refrain from reminding him that he was a street sweep, not a bodyguard for the patrician. But then Teraverre was a city of rules, not like Damsport, where skiving from work was very much the done thing, if you could pull it off. "What time you finishing?"

"Six."

"Fine, I'll see you here at six, and you can take me to your old Ma then."

Two Planks broke into a wide smile. "Yes, alright."

He returned to his focused sweeping of the street. Adelma watched him for a time, until a shiver reminded her that the temperature hadn't risen, and she still had bare arms. Better to wait below decks in her boat with the jute bags over her shoulders than stand in the wind.

All in all, it was proving quite a successful day. She made her way back to the docks, her mind roaming back over her arrival to Teraverre. From there, they drifted to her departure from Damsport.

She'd studiously avoided thinking about Radish after that initial part of the journey, but now that time had passed, she found she didn't mind thinking of him as much. She didn't feel quite so angry about it all.

Seeing him so angry had been quite the shock at the time. She hadn't thought he had it in him to lose his temper like that—it was a welcome surprise, though. It made him more at her level.

Something else occurred to her. If he got so angry, that meant he cared. Unlike all the other nonsense he'd said in the past, somehow that felt more real and less scary. She smiled at the memory of him losing his rag. Maybe she liked the fact that he'd been so upset. And yes, maybe it might be nice to see him again when she got back. Maybe.

She had time to consider anyway—there was the whole journey back. Going to look for him was a whole other matter entirely, though and one that she wasn't prepared to entertain. He would have to come looking for *her*.

Seeing him again, though… She thought of the nights spent at his place and grinned to herself. *Well, that wouldn't be so bad.*

CHAPTER

14

At six, Adelma returned to find Two Planks waiting for her. His broom was gone, and he looked awkward, like he didn't know what to do with his hands.

"You're here," he said, looking surprised.

"Well, yeah. I said I'd come at six."

Two Planks nodded enthusiastically. "Yes, and then you came. Alright, come on, let's go see my old Ma."

Adelma followed him through the streets. They reached a part of town that, although clean and neat, was far less attractive than the rest.

"This way." Two Planks pushed a door in an ugly, squat building. Beyond, there was no light. A staircase stretched up in the dark without a window or an alchemical globe to light the way.

Adelma held the door open behind her for a moment, and then she let it go as she followed. The light shrank back and was eventually swallowed up by the closing door.

The darkness wasn't absolute. There was a vague, watery greyness filtering down from higher up. Two

Planks walked up confidently, and Adelma followed, with both hands ready by her axes—just in case. She didn't think Two Planks was trying to pull anything shifty, but she wasn't the blindly trusting kind, either.

The first-floor landing was more lit up, as light leaked out of a half-opened door at the end of the corridor. Smells of food drifted out with the light. Two Planks headed for the open door.

He pushed it open, revealing a large, bright room with several windows. The sunlight spilling in was the only pleasant thing about the room.

It was crammed with so many triple bunk beds that it was only just possible to walk between them. Laundry lines hung from hooks jammed into the ceiling or stretched diagonally between bunks. Piles of rubbish were stacked neatly at the foot of several beds, adding an unpleasant, sickly smell to the air.

The windows each had a narrow slat at the top, which opened for ventilation. All the slats were open as wide as they could go, but the room still smelt of too many people, of too much breath, sweat, and food, but not enough air. Two Planks squeezed his massive bulk through the maze of bunks, pushing the laundry aside to pass. Adelma caught sight of a couple of people sitting on bunks—they weren't Teraverri. This was clearly Teraverre's clean and organised answer to the migrant worker slum.

"Ma," Two Planks said, approaching a top bunk on which a tiny woman sat.

Adelma felt a brief spike of surprise as she realised the woman looked just like Adelma's mental image of her own mother. Small, just as her Da had described her. A kind, open face. Dark eyes and a small nose. Given Two Planks's size, Adelma had expected a larger woman.

The woman looked up from the shirt in her hands, which she had been sewing a button onto with obviously expert hands. Her face broke into a smile as she caught sight of her son.

"I made a friend, Ma," Two Planks said.

"I'm Adelma." She stuck out her hand.

The woman smiled and shook it. "Dina. You have the look of a Damsian. Oh, it's always good to see someone from home. How did you meet my Slothum?"

"In the street, earlier today. I actually had a business proposition for him—for both of you—and being a wise man, he suggested I should talk to you about it first."

Two Planks nodded. "I don't take no business decision without my old Ma."

"Old, old. It's heavy work raising such a handsome, smart boy." Dina smiled, her eyes crinkling at the corners. She took Two Planks's cheeks in both her hands as she spoke. She barely had to reach down—his head was level with the top bed in the triple bunk.

"Now then," she said, releasing him and turning to Adelma. "What's this about business?"

"Where can we talk private-like?" Adelma asked. "This is sensitive." She jerked her chin in the direction of the workers resting in the other bunks.

Dina nodded. "In the stairwell would be best. I can't be away from my work too long. We've got no light in here, and I have to finish this pile before sunset." She patted the clothes.

The three of them headed out. It was almost a relief to get back to the dark corridor. The room was claustrophobic—Adelma dreaded to think what it was like at night once everyone was back from work.

Dina sat on the top step of the stairwell, and Two Planks took a seat several steps down. His mother patted his hair in a way that made it clear this was a familiar position for them. If not for the giant size of the man, they would almost look like a mother about to tell her son a bedtime story.

For a brief moment, Adelma found herself wondering what it would have been like to have a mother like that—a mother who would have stroked her hair and told her stories.

Adelma pushed the thought away. Her Da had told her all the stories she'd needed, and he'd done a fine job at preparing her for life. He was the reason she was so resourceful and self-reliant now.

"Two Planks said you're trying to get back to Damsport," she began. "Could be I have a way to arrange that for you."

Dina looked at her sharply. "If you're trying to scam us and ask for money—"

"I ain't in the scamming business," Adelma interrupted. "And I ain't looking for money. I need work from you." She took a breath. "I'm in the *smuggling* business."

Dina raised both her eyebrows. "Go on…"

"You do this job for me, I bring you both back to Damsport and make sure that you're both set up either with work or with enough money to tide you over until you get work coming in." Adelma had no real idea how much the Widow would pay her, so she didn't want to promise huge sums. But making sure they were set up— that, she could most definitely handle.

Adelma saw longing in Dina's eyes, and she remembered what Two Planks had said about his mother wanting to leave. Adelma couldn't blame her—she disliked Teraverre, and she'd barely been here for a day.

"That's a deal I'd be very interested in making," Dina said softly. "Life's so expensive here that any money we make is only just enough to live day to day. It's so hard keeping our heads above water, there's no chance of us saving the money we need to pay for our passage back."

Adelma nodded. She wasn't surprised, given the prices she'd seen. Teraverre was the kind of place where earning lower wages would never offer the chance of building up to anything. She felt an odd sense of protectiveness at finding two Damsians trapped in this position. Poor Damsians in Damsport didn't bother her, but poor Damsians stuck in some foreign place felt wrong for some reason.

"I'm a woman of my word," she said. "You do this job for me, and I promise I'll sort you out."

Dina's eyes shone, and her breath hitched. "Home."

"Ma's been wanting to go home long as I can remember," Two Planks said, patting his mother's knee.

Dina looked Adelma in the eye. "You've got a deal. What's the work?"

"You know the quarantine area?"

Dina nodded. Two Planks was looking up at her, and he quickly nodded, too, matching her.

"Could be I need someone to get something from in the sea near the quarantine area and deliver it to an address in Teraverre." Adelma paused. It was one thing for her to risk her life. It was another for her to ask someone else to. "I noticed that nobody pays any attention to the migrant workers who clean the street and take care of the rubbish."

She'd kept an eye out for that on the walk to and from the docks—all the street sweeps were ignored, no matter their nationality.

"I see where you're going with this," Dina said.

Adelma grinned. "Well don't that make life a whole lot easier." She turned serious. "Before I go any further, I need to make something clear." She looked at them both, briefly wondering whether she was making the right decision in trusting them. But her gut was loud and clear on this matter, and she always followed her instincts. "Nothing can go beyond the three of us."

"That goes without saying," Dina replied.

"Yeah, exactly, without saying," Two Planks echoed.

Adelma nodded. "I'd rather say, though, and make it clear. I'm trusting you two. If you don't want to get involved, you can tell me now. I ain't gonna force you or nothing. But if I tell exactly what I need, then you're in. You can't talk to no one, and you don't get to just walk away. This *has* to remain a secret." She realised that a part of her now wanted to threaten them into silence—it was her Da's voice, reminding her that she could only trust herself, her own strength, and him.

But the thought of threatening Dina and Two Planks made her spit taste sour. Two Planks rested his big head against Dina's side, while she had a hand on his shoulder. They looked comfortable and happy together, and Adelma just couldn't bring herself to trample all over that moment with threats of physical violence. That, and it clashed with that odd sense of protectiveness she'd felt not a moment ago.

The world ain't a kind place, my girl. You gotta be able to trust yourself fully. But the rest… You can only trust yourself and your old Da in life, and that's a fact.

"We've got no one to talk to anyway," Dina said, yanking Adelma out of her thoughts. "Not that we would. I give you my word. You can trust us."

Adelma made a snap decision, silencing her father's voice. Her gut wanted to trust Dina, and if Adelma trusted herself fully, then her instincts had to be right.

"I'm glad to hear it. Because what I'm dealing with here, is…" She lowered her voice to a whisper. "Opium."

"What?" Dina whispered back, eyes wide in shock. "You know the penalty…"

Adelma nodded.

"What's opium?" Two Planks asked.

"It's… It puts people to sleep," Dina replied. "It's bad. You have to stay away from it, or you'll sleep for a real long time."

"Like the sleeping prince story?" Two Planks asked.

"Exactly like that." Dina turned back to Adelma. "Why would you take such a risk?"

"Because smuggling's all I've got." Adelma paused, surprised by her answer. And yet it felt right. If she didn't become a smuggler, then all she had was the remains of the life she'd shared with her father. Smuggling would bring a new start.

Of course, there was also Radish. Adelma frowned to herself, surprised that she would think of Radish at this time.

"So, are you in?" she asked.

Dina scanned her face. "We do this, I handle the delivery, not my boy."

"I can do it, Ma," Two Planks said. "Thick as Two Planks, remember—strong, I am. You're small now, and getting smaller every day."

Dina stroked his hair, and Two Planks smiled with genuine pleasure.

"It won't be heavy, love," Dina said. "Strength isn't what's needed here. Did I ever tell you the story of the giant and the pixie?"

Two Planks's eyes shone with excitement. "No."

"Well, there was this magical stone—only a little stone. Like a pebble. Even though it was small as you like, almost as small as you were as a baby, the mighty giant couldn't carry it. He could barely lift it from the ground. He tried and groaned and grunted, and yet he could only lift it an inch or two before he had to let go. But when the little pixie came along, she could lift it without trouble. Because, you see, the stone was magic and could only be picked up by a very specific person. This is the same. What Adelma needs picking up would be light for me, but far too heavy for you."

Two Planks nodded gravely. "I understand." He turned to Adelma. "I won't be able to help you, then. But you can't have better than my old Ma. She's the absolute best. She'll be the right person to carry your magical stone."

Dina also turned to Adelma. "If something happens… If things go wrong… The deal needs to still apply. You must promise to make arrangements to take my Slothum back irrespective of the outcome. That's the only way I'll do it. I do the delivery, and whatever happens, my boy goes back to Damsport."

Two Planks shook his head. "Ma, I ain't no way going home without you."

"I know, love." Dina patted his arm. She gave Adelma a deliberate look and raised an eyebrow in question.

Adelma nodded. "You have my word. Whatever happens." It occurred to her that she could just bring them both back with her now. She was headed back to Damsport anyway, and if the three of them put up with being a bit hungry, she could just about stretch her supplies to get them home.

But if she did that, she had no plan for the Widow. That would mean putting a cross on becoming a smuggler. Unless she could convince Radish to go into business with her. She had a ship, and he had contacts. Between the two of them, they could set something up nice and easy.

That she'd even had that thought was deeply, deeply troubling.

"Adelma?" Dina asked, frowning.

"Yes. Don't worry. All will be fine. Can you swim?" Dina nodded. "Then we should be just fine."

CHAPTER
15

The first thing Adelma did upon reaching Damsport was go to the Old Girl's Arms. The journey had given her plenty of time to think, and the idea of simply asking Radish to go into business together and of bringing Two Planks and Dina back to Damsport without requiring work from them wouldn't leave her alone. It made her stomach churn, and she felt light-headed, like she might throw up any moment. In short, she needed some ale.

"Kriss," she all but gasped on entering. It was so early in the day, Kriss hadn't even finished setting up yet. "I need a drink. A proper drink."

Kriss frowned. "What's wrong?"

Adelma didn't reply right away, taking several deep gulps of the mug of ale Kriss had handed her without fussing over Adelma borrowing the tankard.

"You heard about Radish." Kriss sighed. "Dammit, I been puzzling about how to break it to you right. Who told you?"

Adelma put down the mug and wiped her mouth with the back of her hand. "What's that about Radish?"

"Oh. You didn't hear?"

Adelma shook her head, frowning.

Kriss grimaced. "Well, I guess this is as good a way as any."

"Spit it out, woman. What is it?" Adelma had gone quite still.

"I saw him out the other day, with this woman…"

"Hold on." Adelma raised a hand. This was a blow that wanted to land, but she wasn't just going to sit there and take it. "I ain't gonna go twisting myself into knots over something like that. Could be a business contact, a relative, a friend—could be all sorts of things. His aunt, maybe."

"Well, given that they were kissing, I really hope it weren't his aunt," Kriss said cautiously. "And, um, not like a quick peck or nothing. *Proper* kissing. For quite some time."

This time, the blow landed square in her stomach. Adelma felt more winded than if she'd received a kick to the guts.

"Adelma? You alright?"

She nodded mutely, not trusting that she would be able to speak.

"I figured you should know," Kriss said. "It happened the day after you left. You two been spending so much time together before you left, and it didn't feel right not to say anything, and…"

"Yep, yep. Good thinking." Adelma's voice sounded hoarse to her own ears. "Good thinking. I'm feeling like a rum all of a sudden. Be a treasure and pour me one, would you?"

The world ain't a nice place, my girl. You can't trust nobody but yourself and your old Da. You gotta be on your toes, or someone will try to take advantage of you.

Kriss returned with a bottle and a small metal goblet. Adelma snatched the bottle and proceeded to drink straight from it. She paused for breath and belched. "I'll owe you for this. Don't worry."

She'd have plenty of money once the Widow took her on as a smuggler. Adelma was a good negotiator, and she was going to be using that to her advantage when she approached the Widow. The thought was calming, as if she'd been drowning just a moment before, but now her feet had found their footing, and she was going to be able to wade out.

"Are you alright?" Kriss asked cautiously.

"I'm fine. I'm good. I'm better than that, even. It's like my vision was clouded, and now it's crystal clear."

And it was centred on two things: get opium into Teraverre to become one of the Widow's smugglers and then destroy Assurak. No more pissing about, wasting time on sentimental nonsense.

All these people trying to make her soft, but she wasn't in the business of making friends or rescuing kittens. She had scores to even out, money to make, and a smuggling career to kick off with a bang.

The whole idea of setting up with Radish was a momentary bout of insanity. What luck he'd shown himself unreliable now, before she made any rash decisions. Her old man had been bang on—as always.

Adelma would do it her way, on her own, just as her Da had taught her. Dina and Two Planks would also toe the line. She would make it very clear to them that if they tried to make trouble for her in any way, things would go much worse than just missing out on a return ticket to Damsport. No more rubbish about not wanting to tread on people's toes.

Treading on toes—*that* was the way Adelma did business. She crushed toes, in fact. She made fists, cracking her knuckles.

"You gonna go look for Radish?" Kriss asked in a low voice.

Adelma snorted. "Why would I do that?" A person who was truly indifferent wouldn't care about what gallivanting Radish did when on his own. And she *was* truly, truly indifferent. Indifference oozed from her pores. She couldn't care less if she tried.

Kriss gave her an odd look. "Only, I thought…"

"Thinking? Why d'you go and do something like that for? Get yourself in trouble, thinking will." Adelma winked and belched again. "Alright, I best be off. I got to get myself a meeting with the Widow."

Nothing was going to delay her smuggling opium into Teraverre now. She rolled her shoulders to try and ease some of the tension building there.

Indifferent, indifferent…

∗∗∗

Adelma was stalking over to Bayog, heading to the Widow's compound, when someone called her name.

"Adelma, hey."

She recognised Radish's voice at once, of course. That didn't mean she was going to slow, let alone stop. She had business to attend to and no time for the likes of him.

"Adelma, wait." He caught up with her and touched her arm.

She yanked herself away as if his touch had burnt her. "Get away from me," she snarled.

Her indifference vanished as fast as piss in the sea now that she was in front of him. She met Radish's eyes and was stunned to see a wide grin spreading on his face.

"You're jealous. You're actually jealous," he said.

Adelma spun away and rushed off.

Radish caught up to her. "Wait, just wait."

She might have been fast, but apparently, he was a match for her. Her punch missed him, and rather than cracking him in the jaw, it only caught his shoulder, which hurt her knuckles a lot more than it hurt him. Unfortunately.

"Adelma, just let me—"

"Get away from me!" she roared. All coherent thought left her then as she launched herself at him. She fought clumsily, more flailing at him than truly attacking. For some reason, she couldn't manage to be conscious of her movements.

Radish dodged or blocked, and she was vaguely aware that he was trying to talk to her. "Alright, Adelma. Alright.

Fair enough. But we need to talk, alright? Listen to me—we need to talk."

She stopped and stood a couple of feet from him, panting heavily. She finally managed to get ahold of herself, reminding herself that she didn't care about whatever excuse he could cook up. She didn't even care if the excuse was real or not. Indifference.

I don't care if the woman were dying and he was giving her standing up mouth-to-mouth. Her Da had been right, and that was all that mattered.

"Adelma?"

She looked away from Radish. She couldn't manage to keep up the indifference when she was looking at him, and she didn't want to lose her rag again. Or worse, feel the awful feeling that lay beneath the anger.

In any case, there was nothing more to be said, and that was that. She walked away without looking at him again.

Adelma reached the Widow's compound and knocked.

A metal peephole slid open, revealing a pair of eyes. "What?"

"I'm here to see the Widow."

"You ain't got an appointment."

Adelma rested her hands on her battle-axes. "I got better—a business proposition. Setting up a dream meet in Teraverre."

Saying the words finally removed the last of her anger, replacing it with a rush of power. She felt strong, confident, *limitless*. And she loved how the jargon for smuggling opium rolled off her tongue so easily.

The man behind the door grunted and slammed the peephole shut. Adelma waited. After a time, the door opened.

She was searched, her axes confiscated. This time, though, she was taken right to the end of the corridor, past the room where she had seen Assurak. She'd more or less forgotten about him these last few weeks, what with all the distractions… Anyway, she was back to her normal clarity of mind now, and he was going to get a nasty, nasty lesson in what happened when someone messed with her. The score was going to get evened out, alright.

Her escort opened a door and told her to wait. Inside, it was gloomy, the windows covered with blinds. Shafts of sunlight slipped in diagonally between the blinds' slats, illuminating showers of dust motes that defied gravity, flowing in swirls and eddies. The air felt moist, and there was a vague, unpleasant smell of decay, like old, damp bandages. Adelma felt her nostrils flare in disgust, but she got a hold of herself, bringing her face to neutral once more.

The room was barely furnished. Large copper bowls, filled with still water, lined the walls. Dead flies dotted the surface of the water. Adelma had heard it said that the Widow believed moistness was good for the skin and for the health, and that she credited her long life to surrounding herself with water at all times.

That was the other source of rumours about the Widow: no one knew how old she was.

Several guards stood at attention along the walls, clasping their hands before them. They and the bowls of water provided the room's only furnishings. Adelma waited without so much as twitching a muscle. Shifting from foot to foot or touching her face would imply that she was weak or nervous, and she was neither of those. Legs slightly apart, thumbs slung through the belt hooks of her leathers, she waited.

Just as her legs were starting to ache, a panel on the wall in front of her swung open. The Widow appeared, sat on a chair so massive, it made her already-small frame appear tiny. The chair came forward with a clattering sound. Whatever wheels or mechanism propelled the chair were hidden by the large wooden frame.

The Widow came to a stop in front of Adelma, and the panel behind her closed. She was buried in a huge, heavy black coat, madness in the sweltering Damsian heat. Her skin had the pallid colouring of someone wasting away from a disease. The black coat only enhanced the paleness. The sickly smell of decay Adelma had noticed on entering had increased, completely filling her nostrils. She repressed the urge to gag.

The Widow watched Adelma silently from behind a pair of dark, tinted optics. The lenses were perfectly round, like two large black coins. Adelma wondered how the hell she could see anything, given the gloom.

As if she'd heard the thought, the Widow quirked an eyebrow and lifted a cigarette to her red-painted mouth. Her lips puckered around the cigarette, her lipstick bleeding into her lip wrinkles. Her black hair was cut just long enough to cover her ears. The strands were ironed so stiff and straight, it looked more like a helmet than hair.

The Widow blew out a mouthful of smoke. A finger's width of ash balanced precariously at the end of her cigarette. If not for the smoking, she would have looked like a corpse. With the awful stench of decay, it gave the impression that she was rotting away within the coat, the heavy fabric working to keep her flesh on her bones.

The Widow continued her silent scrutiny, and Adelma bore it without moving or fidgeting, keeping her eyes focused on the black optics. It felt like some kind of standoff or test, and Adelma was determined to pass it with flying colours. She wasn't going to look away like some submissive.

Her legs and arms were starting to grow stiff, having not moved a fraction since she'd first entered the room, but she was used to physical discomfort from her days of fishing.

"Well, then. Talk to me about opium," the Widow said, her voice like the dry crackling of paper.

Adelma finally shifted, and she felt the energy in the room change, relaxing a fraction. She was growing used to the smell too, which was still foul, but no longer quite so nauseating.

"Nobody smuggles it into Teraverre," she said.

The Widow gave the tiniest nod.

"I figured how to do it," Adelma said, careful not to sound cocky. Arrogance was for the incompetent. A real, professional smuggler would state the facts plainly. "So I'm here to offer you a business partnership. My method isn't something that can be replicated regularly, so I can't offer you a real route into Teraverre. Instead, I have a deal for you. I'm in search of employment. *Proper* employment. I do a one-off dream run to Teraverre for you, and if I pull it off, you agree to hire me as part of your smuggling operation."

The Widow took a drag of her cigarette. The ash trembled, but held. "Mighty generous of you. And why would you offer me this deal rather than smuggle opium for your own account? Good money to be made for someone who can get opium into Teraverre"

"Two reasons." Adelma held up two fingers. "Firstly, I want in on your network. I ain't interested in a one-off job, no matter how much money I can make. I wanna be established as one of your smugglers, handling all your most valuable routes. If I can smuggle into Teraverre, that should be proof enough of my skill and put me at least at the level of your top guys, if not above them."

"Hmmm." The Widow took a drag of her cigarette, and the ash crumbled onto her coat.

"Widow," a man said, bursting into the room. It was Assurak. "I heard you're considering doing business with this great cow. It would be a huge mistake." Assurak glared at Adelma, who only just managed not to laugh at him.

He was so small. So pitiful. She would *crush* him.

"And this is my second reason for offering you this deal," Adelma told the Widow.

"Ah." The Widow sounded mildly interested. "Yes I heard about this whole affair between the two of you." It was impossible to tell what she made of it.

"Just so we're clear, this all began when Assurak decided to interrupt my drinking at the Rising Kraken and insult me for my appearance," Adelma said. The Widow might have been told some version of events that Assurak had cooked up, although it was likely that she had enough ways to get information that she would have heard of the real events. "I knocked his lights out for it—which as far as I'm concerned, means we're even. Then he goes and puts a black mark against my name so I can't get no smuggling work nowhere. Well, as I see it, the balance is off again, and I gotta put it right. So, if I can take opium into Teraverre, I don't just want to work on your best routes after that. I want all of *his* routes." Adelma pointed at Assurak. "He tried to take my livelihood, so I take his."

Assurak made an incredulous, spluttering sound.

"Quiet," the Widow snapped.

"You cannot seriously consider her offer," he protested. "She's an untrained, untested smuggler. Hell, she's not even a smuggler yet!"

"If she gets opium into Teraverre for me, she'll have managed what you and all the others have failed to do so far." The Widow's voice was like nails on a chalkboard.

Assurak flinched. He gave Adelma a malevolent glance, but she let it slide off her.

The Widow smoked in silence for a while, considering. Neither Adelma nor Assurak interrupted her. Finished with her cigarette, the Widow flicked it to the ground. One of her goons stepped forward at once, snapping open a silver cigarette case. The Widow grabbed a cigarette, and the goon lit it for her.

"Assurak, I think you should leave," she croaked.

He paled. "But…"

"I'm not in the habit of negotiating my orders," the Widow grated. "This business between the two of you is messy, and I don't want any part in it. And I've had enough of your personal, petty vendettas against people— it's sloppy and bad for business."

"You cannot consider her offer seriously, though."

"As I said, if she gets opium into Teraverre, how could I not? And if she fails, well, your business with her will be concluded anyway. Now *leave*."

Assurak gave Adelma a look of pure loathing. She didn't just let it slide off her—she fed off his hatred. It made her feel stronger, powerful. She was going to ruin him to nothingness. Turn him to little more than a shell of a man.

He left the room after that, closing the door behind him.

"Let's get one thing clear," the Widow creaked. "I don't want to hear about you starting up another of these fights with one of my people. I don't care how justified you think you are. If not for your offer regarding Teraverre, I would have had you taken care of myself for causing a fuss. I don't like *mess*."

Adelma knew better than to protest like Assurak had, but all the same. She had only been doing what was *right*, dammit. "Fine. Let's talk terms and money if I succeed."

The Widow went over the kind of money Assurak earned for his smuggling routes. Adelma did her best to keep her face neutral. That was going to set her up for life. With that kind of spending power, in time, she'd be able to afford a larger ship and a crew. She'd be the head of a *real* smuggling crew. A shiver of excitement ran down her spine. A real smuggling crew and Assurak destroyed— what more could she want?

A small voice piped up, reminding her of one thing, or rather one person she *had* wanted, but she quashed it immediately.

"I'll need some funds up front for the Teraverre venture," she said instead.

The Widow shook her head. "You will take care of any setup costs. And I'll sell you the opium at a good rate."

"You're expecting me to buy the opium? No way. I'm already taking all the risk."

"That's what smugglers *do*—take risks. I'm not in the business of holding hands. I'm in the business of business, and I'm not sending off merchandise with an untested smuggler. All I have is your say-so that you can get opium into Teraverre, but I have no guarantees. For all I know you might just get robbed by pirates on the way. Or you'll pull a fast one on me and try to deal the opium yourself somewhere else. People are unreliable, girl, and I only rely on them once they've proven themselves to me. If you're not happy with that, the door's behind you."

Adelma ground her teeth, but she couldn't argue with that logic. It was the same approach she used. But the cost of the trip, the opium, of decoy merchandise, of the potion to make her look suitably sick, and of course of making the container and device to keep it hidden from sight under the sea… She already didn't have much money left.

Walking away without a deal, though, that wasn't an option. She had her plan, and she was sticking to it. There were *no* alternatives that she was willing to consider. None at all. Her mind wasn't cooperating, though, attempting to again bring Radish into the mix.

"I'll have contracts drawn up," the Widow said. "Confirmation of exactly which smuggling routes you'll be given and the kind of money you'll be looking at. I'll also pay you a handsome bonus to get you setup with a proper ship and crew."

Adelma gave a small smile. She would be a *real* smuggler then. She made fists. No alternatives—this was her only option. Once again, her mind felt clear, her path simple, stretching straight out in front of her. She would have to bankrupt herself to afford the trip and probably sell everything she owned, other than her Da's boat, but what the hell. If she couldn't make the trip to Teraverre work, she'd be dead anyhow, and then she wouldn't care about money.

But she *would* make it work. And she would do it *alone*. Once she'd succeeded, she would owe nothing to no one, and no one would be able to get to her.

"Fine. And I also want a refund for all the money I spend up front."

"That goes without saying."

The two women exchanged a long, silent look. Adelma felt a shiver—this felt like the start of something big. A partnership with the Widow Bones.

"I'll give you the details of my contact in Teraverre," the Widow said. "He'll take delivery of the goods, and he will send me confirmation that they have been received. If you tell him you've made a full delivery and there's so much as a pinch missing, it'd be best for your health never to set foot in Damsport again."

Adelma frowned. "What you taking me for? Some two-bit rip-off merchant? On top of which, you're making me buy the opium. I'll do what I want with it—lucky for you, what I want is to deliver it to your contact."

The Widow showed her teeth, and Adelma wasn't sure if it was a threat or a smile. "I like you. You have spirit."

Smile, then. "Can't reciprocate the feeling for now—you're asking me to sink into a financial hole to make this plan work."

"But the reward will be worth your while. And if you need any fake paperwork, that, I can arrange."

Adelma nodded. "That's the least you can do." It was probably stupid to talk back to the Widow, but Adelma couldn't bring herself to care. She felt reckless, lightheaded.

The Widow gave something between a cough, a wheeze, and a laugh, and she leaned forward. "So tell me, I'm curious. How will you get my opium into Teraverre?"

"I ain't telling no one that—least of all someone what has smugglers working for her."

The Widow leaned back. "Fine. I can live with that, so long as you make the delivery." She waved her cigarette in the air, and Adelma heard the sound of a door opening behind her.

"Out you go," the man who had escorted her earlier grunted.

Adelma frowned. "But I need the paperwork, the details of the—"

"I'll be supplying you with that," the man said.

The Widow's massive chair made a clacking noise as it came to life. The panel behind her swung open, and the chair rolled back out.

"Pleasure doing business with you," Adelma called.

There was no reply from the Widow, and Adelma followed the escort out. They had almost reached the main door when Assurak popped out of one of the rooms along the long corridor.

"Aw, you were waiting to see me out?" Adelma asked with mock coyness. "So nice of you."

"You made a massive mistake," he snarled.

Adelma wiped the smile from her face and allowed herself to tower over him. She was a head taller, and she glared down at him. "No, *you* did, the day you bothered me at the Kraken. A huge error on your part."

"By the time this is over, you're going to regret ever setting eyes on me," Assurak threatened.

"Funny, that's exactly how *you'll* feel when I'm done with *you*." Adelma jabbed him in the chest with her finger. "And if you bother me while I go about preparing my trip, remember that nice shiner I gave you before. I could wipe the floor with you anytime I choose."

"I will *destroy* you," Assurak whispered.

A heavy hand grabbed Adelma's shoulder. "Enough. The Widow doesn't like fights," the escort said. "Take your weapons and go."

As Adelma walked home, the adrenaline from the meeting seemed to wear off, and she suddenly felt exhausted. She wanted to collapse in bed and sleep for several days. And she planned on doing just that, because once she started getting everything ready, there likely wouldn't be much sleep for her.

It wasn't until she was in her bedroom, about to drop into her bed, that another bedroom—one with whitewashed walls, dark exposed beams, and an irritating bedside table—flashed into her mind. She pushed the image away and fell into sleep.

CHAPTER 17

Adelma took a few more weeks to get everything ready. Time passed in a kind of ultra-focused blur. She did another trip to Teraverre to meet with the Widow's contact and check where the delivery would be taking place.

Then she went to Two Planks and Dina to finalise the details with them. She supplied Dina with a ring-shaped lifebuoy that would make it easier for the woman to swim back with the opium container. Two Planks passed within sight of the quarantine dock every day for his sweeping job, so he'd let Dina know once Adelma had managed to get in. They would then simply keep careful watch of the ship to see when it left, and the two week countdown to retrieving the container would then begin from that moment.

While Adelma was at it, she also did a little *leaning* on Dina and Two Planks to make it clear what would happen if they blabbed to anyone about any of this.

Adelma more or less managed to ignore the hurt and disappointment in Dina's eyes. Business was business, and she was done being soft and having people take advantage.

She also set about selling every last item she possessed to raise the money she needed. A few things of no value that she couldn't bear to part with, she stored on her Da's boat. Her Da's comb—he was quite neat with his hair, until he fell sick—and the couple of books he liked to read. They were dog-eared and creased, their pages yellow and musty with age.

That done, she put the house up for sale. By that point, the house was just a shell, after all. Still, selling it felt as heavy and difficult as hefting a granite boulder up a hill. Adelma found herself breathing deeply, standing in the middle of her living room, paralysed for a moment. After the house went, all she would have left in the world was her boat and the few belongings inside it.

She raised her chin. And that was fine. She had a plan, and she was going to see it through no matter what.

The sale happened quickly—properties right on the docks were desirable. And then just like that, her old life was gone. Gone as gone.

That day, she bumped into Radish again. She kept seeing him about town, and he still hadn't given up trying to talk to her. Adelma was growing good at completely drowning out his voice, as if he weren't there. Her mind was too completely focused on the job at hand to have even the tiniest bit of spare space for the likes of him. Nothing mattered but her opium run.

She saw Assurak from time to time, too. Him, she didn't walk away from, but instead confronted square on. He couldn't afford to interfere with her and risk earning the displeasure of the Widow, so he always had to back down, which was ever so satisfying. His threats were just empty words that he couldn't follow through on, and Adelma experienced immense pleasure at reminding him just what would happen if the Widow heard he'd messed up an opium run into Teraverre.

One of the last things she saw to was the potion that would make her look sick. She was actually struggling on the money front. The funds from the house sale and the rest were only just about enough to cover her costs so far—she wouldn't have enough to pay for the potion.

So she headed to the alchemist who used to make her Da's pain-killer. The shop was little more than a square room crammed with shelves, drawers, and bottles. The only window was hidden behind a floor-to-ceiling metal cabinet divided into a myriad of little drawers, each with its own scrawled label. With no natural light, the single alchemical globe overhead cast a yellow glint.

"Morning," Adelma said, closing the door behind her.

The alchemist was behind his counter, working on something. The man looked no different than Adelma remembered. Wild, frizzy hair shot out around his head in corkscrew curls. Thick optics magnified his eyes. A heavy leather apron with much scarring and splotching, combined with the wild hair, always made him look like he had just escaped from a nasty alchemical explosion.

Adelma crossed the narrow space to the counter. The yellow light gleamed off glass bottles and jars. One of them contained tiny skulls, another held eyes. The alchemist was hard at work dissecting a frog.

"I said *morning*," Adelma repeated, placing both hands on the counter.

"Do you know the effects of filtering a condensed boutose broth through the lungs of a frog?" the alchemist asked, lifting a pair of tiny lungs from the frog's body and examining them.

Frowning, Adelma looked down at the poor animal. She hoped it had been dead before the man began his experiment.

"What can I do for you?" he asked, putting the lungs down in a glazed ceramic dish.

"I need something from you, and the way I look at it, you owe me."

"I *owe* you?" The alchemist raised an eyebrow at her.

The first time Adelma had come looking for the painkiller for her Da, she'd been so emotional over the state her father was in, she hadn't even remembered to negotiate. The alchemist had royally ripped her off on the price.

When she'd returned feeling more clear-headed, he'd refused to budge on the price. Her father insisted that she get exactly the same pain-killer, from the same man, and he wouldn't hear of her going to another place for something similar. So as not to add to his worries, Adelma hadn't told him that she was getting ripped off, but it left her in a tricky position.

The alchemist knew she needed him more than he needed her, so he didn't need to lower the price to keep her custom. She was forced to cough up every time her Da wanted the pain-killer. That plus the doctor visits had sunk Adelma and her Da into debt at the end.

And more importantly, it had deeply, deeply rankled Adelma to have someone rip her off repeatedly like that. That score needed to be evened out.

So she reached across the counter, grabbed him by the shirt front, and hauled him up on the counter, sending a few glass vials smashing to the ground along with the poor dissected frog. The shirt was cheap, and it tore, so Adelma had to re-adjust her grip to be holding on to his apron.

"Let's get something straight. You ripped me off repeatedly over my old man's pain-killer, and you know it. So yeah, you owe me. You're gonna make me something that will make me look sick for a time—very sick. Sick enough to scare people into thinking I'm contagious, so they'll send me straight to the quarantine dock when my ship enters port. And you'll do it for free."

"If you think you can scare me—"

"How valuable is your shop to you?" Adelma snarled. "I'm levelling the score with you whether you cooperate or not. You don't do this for me, and I'm going to destroy your whole shop."

The alchemist squeaked in panic as she drew one of her battle-axes, raising it so the blade was level with his face.

"Your whole shop. You screwed me over when you knew my old man was dying slowly and painfully. I think losing your livelihood is about fair. Or you help me."

"I'll help. I'll help."

Adelma grunted and threw him to the ground. He fell awkwardly with a cry. "See that you do. I want something that will take effect quickly, but only lasts a few hours or so. I need to look real sick. Spectacular sick. Think throwing-up-all-over-my-boat's-deck kind of sick. Here's a list of possible symptoms I need to be showing." She slammed a list Mercy had written for her on the counter.

The alchemist glanced down at the list. "I can do that easily."

"And I'll be leaving your name with a friend of mine. Anything bad happens to me, they'll come to you for answers, and it won't be pleasant. Got it?"

The alchemist nodded jerkily. "Of course, I'm a reputable...There's no need for anything."

The threat was more about being thorough in following her Da's approach than something Adelma actually felt like she needed. The alchemist stank of fear, and she knew his type well. He was a petty bully who liked to screw those who were less powerful than him, but he lacked the backbone to actually confront someone head on.

"I'll be back to pick it up tomorrow. Make sure it's ready."

Adelma grinned as she left. Evening scores felt damned good. When she took over Assurak's smuggling runs, it was going to feel bloody *amazing*.

***

That night, Adelma looked around her at the neatly packed decoy merchandise in the hull of her boat. Hidden among it, in a false-bottomed crate was the container for the opium. If she'd been able to buy opium at that price back when she was smuggling with Kieran, she would have made a killing.

The Widow had sold it to her at cost, which Adelma grudgingly had to admit was fair. If she'd had any previous dealings with the Widow, she might have been able to get the opium for free, but no matter. There'd be plenty of money once the job was successful.

All doubts about risking her life had completely left her. She knew in her bones her plan would work, and she felt absolutely no fear. Her Da was with her on this—of that, she was also sure. The thought was comforting.

She grabbed her Da's favourite book. It had always looked odd, almost like a toy in the big man's hands, but he'd loved to read, something Adelma hadn't gotten from him. She ran her hands over the spine.

"Hope you're proud of me, Da," she whispered. It felt right that he would be coming with her on her first big job as a smuggler. "Wish you could be here to see it all." Tomorrow, she would pick up her potion from the alchemist and set off. The first day of her new life.

Another image flashed in her mind, of Dina and Two Planks in the stairwell, with Two Planks resting his large head against his tiny mother's knees. With a frown, Adelma put the book back in its place. Best to just focus on the job at hand.

Above decks, the clear night sky stretched out, limitless, punctured by stars. She'd set up her hammock, and she settled herself into it, feeling it sway softly beneath her. She propped her head up on her left arm and grabbed her bottle of rum. It must have been somewhere near three in the morning, but she didn't feel tired at all. She would sleep later, once she was out at sea and well on her way to Teraverre.

Adelma heard a creak, something out of place among the gentle sounds of the dock at night. She sat up, immediately alert. Had it come from her boat? It hadn't been far, whatever it was.

The silence continued. A small alchemical globe hung from a hook at the mast of her boat. The light was enough for her to see her deck clearly, and the moon overhead was bright. Still, she saw no one, and the dock beyond was deserted. She didn't relax, though, turning to look at the neighbouring ships.

Someone there, maybe? Adelma cursed herself for having used an alchemical globe and ruining her night vision. *Stupid, stupid.* She killed the light and waited some more.

When nothing else happened, she decided it must have been nothing. Sometimes ships were burgled at night, but she wouldn't make an interesting target since her ship was clearly a fishing boat. The fact that she was on deck would also deter any would-be robbers.

She was once again looking up at the stars, when she heard the unmistakable sound of a boot hitting wood—the wood of her deck specifically. She leapt out of her hammock, drawing her battle-axes. Something swung through the air, followed by a tinkle of broken glass as whatever it was fell through the trapdoor that led below decks.

With a whoosh, heat and the smell of smoke rose up from the inside of the boat.

"No!" Fear unlike anything Adelma had experienced before gripped her. Her boat was on fire.

The shadow who had thrown the glass container jumped off her boat and sped off down the dock. Adelma didn't even try to give chase. She vaulted onto the docks, sprinting to the alarm bell. She rang the code for fire.

"Fire!" She bellowed before releasing the bell and running back. She dropped her axes on the dock so her hands would be free.

She had a bucket and rope aboard, but a fire down in the hull would need the help of the firemen if it had any chance of being put out. She lowered the bucket at the end of its rope to fill it with seawater.

Once it was full, she grabbed it and headed below decks. The fire was already blazing strong, devouring the rolls of fabric that made up her decoy cargo. Adelma's bucket was as effective as a child pissing on the flames. She turned back when hands appeared at the trapdoor, handing her a bucket of seawater.

The alarm had been heard. More boots rang out on the deck. She grabbed the bucket and flung the water on the flames. More voices and footsteps sounded overhead as a chain formed and more buckets of water made their way to her.

The smoke was fast becoming overwhelming. Adelma coughed, her eyes and throat burning. No matter how many buckets of water she poured on the flames, they didn't seem to die. They disappeared for a moment, dampened, before slowly flickering back to life.

Her boat was disappearing before her eyes, swallowed up by the black smoke. "No," Adelma croaked, throwing yet another ineffectual bucket of seawater. Her lungs felt like they were full of metal shavings that burned and scraped her raw.

A portion of the deck collapsed in front of her, sending embers and burning pieces of wood everywhere. She took a step back, protecting her face with her right arm.

Her boat. Her Da's boat.

It was an inferno. The flames engulfed everything, some bursting up through the ragged hole in the deck. Adelma felt hypnotised, unable to tear her eyes away from the flames.

Her boat. Her Da's boat. Her Da's boat.

A wailing siren told her of the arrival of the firemen.

"More water!" she croaked, but the buckets had stopped coming. Someone somewhere shouted. Footsteps ran overhead.

She finally got her senses back, and she darted forward, through the flames to where the opium container was hidden. The heat was unbearable, and Adelma's hands fumbled clumsily with the false bottom, struggling to open it. Finally, though, her hands closed on the opium container. The false bottom of the crate had protected it.

Coughing and spluttering, she tried to make her way back to the ladder. The smoke filled her mouth, her nostrils, and her lungs.

Hands grabbed her arms, pulling her up. She was yanked out into the clean night air, her lungs gasping in the fresh air. Everything inside her felt like it had been rubbed with sandpaper.

Water sprayed her face, and as hands dragged her off her boat, she saw a powerful fire hose dousing the flames below decks. It all seemed to be happening in slow motion. Adelma could see the water, hear the hissing of the flames, and smell the smoke, and yet she felt like she wasn't really here.

Her hands felt numb while her eyes burned. She clung to the opium container, both her arms wrapped around it.

"Are you alright?"

Adelma blinked over at the person who had asked this. She wasn't surprised to see Radish—nothing could surprise her, not now that she had seen her father's boat burning.

He ran a hand on the side of her face. "You've got almost no eyebrows left. Your hair had started to catch fire when I pulled you out."

Adelma didn't answer. Couldn't answer.

"What happened?" Radish asked.

"Someone threw something down the hatch. Something made of glass. Then the fire started." She blinked again, turning back to her ship.

A gaping hole in the deck, ringed with smouldering wood, spewed flames towards the sky. More flames crawled up the mast. The hose seemed to dampen the fire temporarily, but then it would start up again.

"It's an alchemical fire," Radish told her. "They've adjusted the hose to alchemically treated water, but…"

Adelma watched as her sails caught fire. Her Da's sails.

"But it's too late," she mumbled.

Adelma awoke to a pounding headache, as bad as any hangover. Her throat and lungs were so raw that breathing hurt. Her eyes felt like they'd been gummed together by something, and her lids parted slowly and painfully. As she sat up, she felt painful burnt patches on her body, and looking down, she could see fresh white bandages.

She sat up slowly and swayed, confused and disorientated. Radish's room looked much the same as before.

My boat. My Da's boat.

She tried to speak, but all that came out was a weak, dry sound. Through the bedroom door, she could see Radish in the living room. He was seated at a table in front of a ledger and some papers, and he looked up at her, his eyes full of concern. The large man looked incongruous, pen in hand like an accountant. Adelma had no real memory of what had happened after he pulled her from her burning boat. Nothing beyond the image of her boat engulfed in flames, which was branded into her mind.

"What…" She blinked groggily. "My boat."

"Brought you home last night. You were in a bad way." Radish grimaced. "There's nothing left of the boat. By the time they got the fire under control, there wasn't enough left to salvage."

Adelma shook her head. The loss left her breathless, but she wouldn't deal with it for now. Couldn't deal. That would be for later.

She looked up at Radish. That she could deal with: he was the last person she wanted help from. She tried to move, but her whole body protested. She hadn't seen him leave his table, but now, he was next to her.

"Easy, easy. It's gonna be painful for a while," he said.

She tried to push him away, but she had all the strength of a newborn—and a weak newborn at that.

"Adelma," Radish sighed. "Enough now. I know you're angry at me, but firstly, you've got nowhere else to go, and secondly, I'm helping you. You're going to have to listen to me explain at some point."

"Kriss said. Not just a quick kiss or nothing." There, it was out in the open.

Radish gave a joyless smile. "Yes. I did that on purpose."

"Great, glad we had that talk." She tried to get out of the bed, but Radish pushed her gently back in place.

"Did it ever occur to you that I have feelings, too?" His voice was its usual low, smooth self, but there was an undertone of tension to it.

"Huh?"

"I had to know, Adelma. Before you left, that argument we had, it really hurt. I'm prepared to put up with all your nonsense if I know that underneath it, there's something real. I was sure there was, but that day, I really didn't know anymore. I'm not a masochist, Adelma, and you've been putting me through the ringer all this time. So I set things up with a friend, making sure that Kriss would see us. I had to know whether you cared or not. Far from my smartest move, I'll give you that, but I wasn't thinking too clearly at that point." Radish smiled then. "And it told me what I needed to know—you got jealous. You care."

Adelma looked at him square in the eye. He looked just the same as before—strong, sturdy, not handsome in a conventional way, but he was handsome to her. And she wanted nothing to do with him. Never again was she putting herself in a position where someone could hurt her like he had. Never. No one would have that kind of power over her again.

She pushed him away with a hand to his chest, and then slowly, painfully, she climbed out of bed. The burnt skin pulled and tugged as she moved, reminding her just how bad the fire had been.

"Adelma, you should stay and rest."

"Not near you, I ain't."

She saw the container she'd rescued from her ship, and she picked it up. She almost cried out from the pain of it, but Radish certainly didn't deserve to hear her pain.

Then she shuffled her way slowly out of the house, towards the Old Girl's Arms. Radish stayed with her the whole way, making sure she didn't stumble and fall—her legs weren't very solid. She didn't want him there, but she didn't have the energy to push him away again. It was all she could do to keep walking and carry the container.

She stumbled into the Old Girl's Arms.

"Aye, Adelma!" Kriss rushed over. "I heard. Are you…"

"Rum," Adelma croaked. "I need to sleep on your floor tonight. And please take this from me."

Kriss nodded quickly, taking the container. "Course—of course." She helped Adelma towards the bar counter, and as she did, she looked over Adelma's shoulder, her face darkening.

"And get him out of here," Adelma added.

"You don't need to tell me twice," Kriss said coldly, still staring at Radish.

"I'm not trying to overstay my welcome," he said, raising his hands in a pacifying gesture. "I'll leave you both to it. But remember what we talked about, Adelma."

After that, everything went very, very blurry. Kriss took Adelma to the back and sat her in a comfortable chair. There was small table next to it, and Kriss put down a bottle of rum.

"I heard about your Da's boat. Adelma, I'm so sorry. I know this ain't much, but if it will help, you can stay here long as you want."

Adelma reached for the rum. That was when the blurriness really got bad. She was vaguely aware of Kriss occasionally appearing in her line of sight. Everything felt numb for a while. At some point, the rum bottle was swapped for a new one, and then finally, blessed darkness enveloped her.

***

Adelma awoke with a pounding hangover. Her tongue was stuck to the roof of her mouth. A hammer had taken up residence inside her skull, pounding against her forehead, while her hair felt like it was growing inwards, strangling her poor shrivelled brain into a painful little raisin. Her eyes were gummed shut. She winced as she peeled one open.

This time, she woke up in Kriss's back room. She shifted, her whole body creaking, but it didn't feel as bad as the previous day. She groaned.

"You're awake," Kriss said from the bar, where by the sound of it, she was setting up for the day. "There's water on the table next to you. And some food."

Numbly, Adelma turned her head, her neck cracking like the knees of an old supplicant. There was a mug there, and sure enough, it was full of water. Adelma took a deep glug, the moisture helping to unstick her tongue from the roof of her mouth. Both felt furry. She finished the water. The food was a huge portion of Big Wendy's famous ginger chicken rice porridge. Adelma wolfed it down, realising that she was starving.

"You're a goddess among women. Have I told you that, Kriss?" she croaked.

"You could probably tell me again." Kriss appeared in the doorway, frowning. "You look like hell, Adelma. You need to take it easy for a while. Stay here as long as you need."

"I don't need a nursemaid," Adelma grunted. She didn't want anyone. She wanted to be alone—completely alone.

"You're welcome," Kriss replied, her raised eyebrow showing her disapproval. "Look, I get that things look bleak right now, but—"

"Don't give me bloody platitudes," Adelma snapped. "You got no idea what that boat meant to me. What it—" She stopped talking abruptly when her voice caught.

Her Da's boat. Her *Da's* boat.

She would never have sunk low enough to cry, but right now, she wanted to. She missed her father like a veteran soldier missed a lost limb. Even though he'd died months ago now. Even though his death had been a blessing. She hadn't cried when he died, and she wasn't about to cry now. Although she was finding it hard to keep the tears at bay.

Her Da had left a hole in her life, and without the boat to fill some of it, that void now yawned open, threatening to consume her with loneliness. And somehow, what had happened with Radish made that feel even worse. She buried her head in her hands.

Kriss made a low soothing sound in the back of her throat, and Adelma felt her perch on the chair's armrest. She placed one hand on Adelma's shoulder.

After a time, Adelma got herself under control again. "I'm gonna go spend time on the docks," she told Kriss roughly, not meeting the woman's eyes.

"Good idea. Also, Mercy sent you a note. She actually came herself to deliver it yesterday, but you'd blacked out. She's worried about you."

Adelma nodded. "I'll go see her later today." She still didn't look at Kriss. "Um, thanks, Kriss. You're a legend. I'll pay you back for it all."

"Don't you dare. Now go to the docks and then to see Mercy. And then come back here for the night."

Adelma headed out, feeling far more solid than she had the previous day. The docks first, and then Mercy.

Watching all those ships was like rubbing salt into the wound, and yet it was soothing at the same time. She didn't move for the rest of the day, watching the ships come and go, floating in her pain and sadness, aching for the loss of her Da's boat.

***

When Adelma reached Mercy's place, she only had to knock once before the door opened.

"No secret knock, eh?" Adelma asked as she stepped into the gloom. "I should lose all my worldly possessions more often."

"Shhh," Mercy hissed, quickly locking the door. "They might be listening."

"Of course."

Once they were settled as comfortably as it was possible to get in Mercy's sitting room, Mercy gave her a once-over. "You look terrible, but not in any danger."

"Sounds about right."

Mercy pulled out a notebook. "This is especially for you. A new notebook for investigations concerning you. I've been leading several detailed enquiries about what happened around you of late. And the first thing is that according to the evidence I gathered, it seems that the display Radish put on was a kind of test of loyalty—"

Adelma snorted. "I don't want to hear it. And if *he* told you that—"

Mercy snapped her head up from her notebook, looking outraged. "As if I *ever* rely on hearsay or opinions. No, this is based on facts." She patted her notebook. "Empirically verifiable *facts*. I had him followed, and the woman in question, too. It seems she's an old friend, and I could find no evidence of any previous relations between them, which made me question the validity of what Kriss had seen. I got testimonials from people who know them both, expressing what seemed like genuine incredulity that anything would be happening between Radish and this woman. I also did a full audit to check whether Radish could have anticipated my investigation and had these people paid off to lie for him. However, my research didn't bring up any evidence of payments or agreements between them. It could be that Radish has a whole network that's more sophisticated than mine. Not beyond the realm of the possible, but rather unlikely. Although it would imply a rather decent sized conspiracy."

Mercy frowned, but her eyes were gleaming. The thought was appealing to her. "Then there is the issue of kissing the woman in public, outside of the Old Girl's Arms, where he knew Kriss would see. The lack of subtlety doesn't support the kind of discrete and careful work required to setup such an extensive network. Instead, it does seem to lean in favour of some kind of display. A test. Now, that kind of behaviour is odd for a courting human male. Uncommon, from what my sources tell me of the average human relationship. However, I did find a species of frog that behaves in a similar way. The frogs mate for life, but early on in the partnership, the male will go and find another female in order to provoke his female into staking her territory—"

"I really don't want to hear about Radish, Mercy."

Mercy peered at her through her jam-jar glasses. "Are you sure? These frogs are fascinating. Once the original female frog stakes her territory—"

"I'm positive."

"Very well. For now. This is important, Adelma. Such information shouldn't be ignored." She turned a few pages in her notebook. "I also investigated what happened to your boat."

"Let me guess. You eventually found a link to Assurak."

"Yes! Did you also look into the shipping schedules, trading patterns, and changes in the way people were drinking?"

"Something like that."

Mercy began to explain the convoluted research she'd done to get to Assurak, detailing the rather large network of contacts Assurak had used so the fire wouldn't be linked to him. Of course, he couldn't have anticipated Mercy.

It gave Adelma time to mull over her next move. Assurak had destroyed her livelihood—at least that's how he would see it. But he'd done more than that since that boat and the cargo inside represented all her worldly possessions, not to mention all that remained of her father.

This was a declaration of war. But she needed to be smart. Killing him now would just put the Widow on her back, and Adelma was realistic enough to know she couldn't take on the Widow by herself. No point getting revenge if she wasn't around to enjoy it. So first, she would have to find a way to get Assurak out of the Widow's good graces. And then…

"What are you doing?" Mercy asked.

Adelma realised with a start that she'd stood up. "Nothing. Just making plans. I need to go ahead with getting the opium to Teraverre. I need to get myself a ship."

"Is that really a good idea? I mean, it's a pretty dangerous job, and you're not in your best state. Maybe you should leave it."

"You didn't have a problem with it before."

"That was before your ship and everything you own went up in flames. Maybe you're not as solid on your own as you like to think. And Teraverre's a dangerous place."

Adelma snorted. "I know what I'm doing."

"Hmm."

Adelma frowned, not sure she liked the implication behind Mercy's tone. "Actually, Mercy, can I ask you a huge favour?" she asked, partly to move the conversation on and partly because she genuinely did need a favour. "I need some information."

Mercy smiled. "Now that, I can do."

"Find out for me which ships are Assurak's, will you? I'm pretty sure he has more than one."

"Consider it done. Why d'you want to know?"

"I need a ship, and I got no more money. I'm broke as a dock rat. So I'll have to steal one, and fair's fair if I steal one from him." Adelma grinned, and just like that, she felt like herself again.

"You'll also need money." Mercy pushed a purse into Adelma's hand.

Adelma looked up at her and frowned. "You mean this is a loan, right?"

"Um, no. You need it. I have it. So…"

"Mercy, while I seriously appreciate the gesture, I don't take charity. I'm paying every last copper bit of this back."

Mercy smiled. "Suit yourself. But in the meantime, put it to good use and get Assurak back."

CHAPTER
19

Before long, Adelma put together a plan to steal Assurak's ship. Mercy delivered as only Mercy could, with a banquet of information about Assurak's four ships. No one would have found it weird for Mercy to be gathering information about that, whereas Adelma asking those questions would have raised eyebrows.

Adelma scoped out the ship she was planning to steal. It was just about small enough for her to manage alone, and since it was supposed to head off in a couple of days, it was packed with supplies for a long trip. In short, the ship was the perfect target.

Adelma had also picked up her potion from the now very subdued alchemist, who assured her she would look as sick as a dog once she drank the concoction. He'd grovelled and apologised—Adelma's point had clearly been heard. *Good.*

With the potion and the opium container, she still had the essentials for her smuggling plan to work, and with

Mercy's money, she could buy the last few things she needed.

Once she was ready, she waited for night to fall. The docks were dark and silent by the time she arrived, the sea gently lapping against the wooden hulls. Adelma slipped quietly along the smooth flagstones, keeping to the shadows. Tucked under her right elbow were the metal rods she'd bought to disable the engine on Assurak's other ships. She didn't want to risk anyone giving chase once she made off with her prize. Under her left arm, awkward and heavy, she carried her opium container. The alchemist's vial was carefully wrapped up in cloth and tucked away in her pocket.

She paused long enough to examine the ship she would be stealing. Two sentries waited above deck, and as she watched, a third stuck his head up from the trapdoor leading below. *Three in total—easily manageable.*

Adelma continued to the far corner of the docks. Waiting in the shadow was the urchin boy she'd paid half a copper earlier that evening. She put a finger to her lips and quietly placed her container down. Then she gently put the metal rods on the floor one by one so they wouldn't clang or roll.

Adelma produced half a silver coin. It winked in the moonlight. "See this?" she asked the boy.

He nodded.

"You get one of those now, one of those later, if you do exactly as I say," she whispered. "You try to steal from me, and you'll get this." She pulled one of her axes from its holder, and its razor-sharp edged gleamed cruelly.

The urchin swallowed audibly. "I don't steal nothing," he protested in a low voice.

"My arse you don't steal nothing. I seen you about the docks before, and you got fingers as sticky as the day is long. Fair's fair—an urchin's gotta live, too—but tonight, what I want you to do is look after my things while I go for a little swim, alright? And I don't want nothing missing when I get back. You're gonna stay here with my leathers, this container, and this vial, and when the temples ring three, you're gonna take them over there—see where the light is, by the crane?"

The boy nodded.

"Good. This vial is worth more than your life. You break it, I break you—got it?"

The urchin nodded almost distractedly. He'd probably heard similar threats from everyone who'd paid him to do small jobs. Urchins could be really useful, until they decided they were better off robbing you than working for your coins.

Adelma stripped carefully. Her burns were healing well, but the skin was still very sensitive. She removed her axes and strapped them back on once she was naked. The last thing she wanted was to have wet clothes get in the way. She also knew she was a startling sight naked, strong as she was. It would shock the sailors when she landed on the deck, enough to give her an advantage.

The urchin gawked at her as she finished setting her axes in place.

"What?" she asked him.

The lad had the sense to shut his mouth. "Nothing."

"Don't worry." Adelma laughed. "They don't all look like me."

And what a shame that was. The world would have been better if more women had hard, flat muscle, rather than soft, rounded curves.

She grabbed her metal rods and headed for the water, tucking them under her left arm. The water was cool and dark as she slipped in, and she revelled in the feel of it over her skin.

Adelma swam like she was born in water—the result of growing up on a ship. She moved slowly, careful not to splash with her metal rods, her strokes smooth but powerful in spite of the awkwardness of carrying something. Her twin axes were a reassuring weight against her thighs, but she was pleased not to have to contend with clothes or boots.

Adelma swam out to the middle of the dock. The moon cast a long reflection that seemed to stretch all the way to the horizon, as if inviting her out. She grinned—in a short while, if all went well, she would be answering that call. Once she was far enough, she turned back, treading water to pick out Assurak's ships.

She would be starting on the one farthest to the left, making her way over to the one she was already beginning to think of as *her* ship. It was called *The Bream*, a good name. *The Bream* was the farthest to the right of Assurak's ships, slimmer than the two heavyweights on either side of it. In the dark, it looked almost black, sleek and shiny as an eel.

Adelma swam slowly. *The Slippery Eel* would be a better name—she would have to rename the ship, remove any remnants of Assurak from it.

When she was close enough to the first ship, she slowed to the swimming equivalent of crawling. Any disturbance in the water would send ripples against the hull, and if the sentries were good, they'd be alert to that kind of thing.

Voices rang out softly over the water—sailors talking the night away.

Adelma took a deep breath and carefully dove under the surface. It was darker than a womb, and Adelma groped blindly for the ship's propeller. She slipped a rod into the propeller fins and kicked her feet to return to the surface. That would ensure the propeller jammed once the engine started up.

She moved on to the next ship. As she groped for the propeller, something painful stung her hand. She jerked back, and as she did, she moved her left arm. A rod escaped.

Adelma kicked a leg out, trying to stop its fall, reaching down with her right hand to catch it. It bounced against her knee and away from her. She groped with her right hand but felt nothing.

Her lungs cried out for air, and she had to kick back to the surface, yelling curses in her head. That jellyfish, or whatever it was, better get crushed under a rock, along with every other member of its miserable species.

Now that she was missing a rod, one of Assurak's ships would be free to chase after her the moment the theft was discovered.

She tightened her grip on the remaining rods and looked at the other ships, trying to gauge which would be the slowest. She cursed a few more times in her head, and then she got back to work.

It was slow going, but she had finally disabled the propeller of two ships, leaving *The Bream* and one other—a bulky thing that would hopefully be too slow to catch up.

She turned to *The Bream*, swimming slowly. Luck was on her side: the two sentries on board were talking. Even better, she could see a golden light on the deck. They obviously had some kind of alchemical globe, which meant their night vision would be worthless. She guessed the third sentry would still be below.

Adelma grabbed hold of one of the rubber fenders hanging off the side of the ship. Slowly, so as not to make a noise, she pulled herself up. Her arms burned from the effort of hauling herself out of the water, but it was a savagely satisfying burn, and she didn't hurry.

One hand, then the other, grabbed hold of the edge of the deck. She now hung off the edge of the ship, part of her legs still dangling in the water.

"That's what I told him, mate… That's what I told him," one of the sentries said.

A glass bottle clinked. They were having a drink.

"Bloody out of order, if you ask me," the other one said.

"Yeah, out of order."

Adelma carefully pulled herself up by her hands, until her head peeked over the edge of the deck far enough to see the two men. They were seated on stools, one with his back to Adelma, the other facing her. But just as she had expected, their night vision was too compromised for him to see her.

She lowered herself back down, giving her arms a moment of respite. She took a deep, slow breath. Then in one rapid movement, she vaulted over the ship's rail and onto the deck.

Landing on the wood, naked and dripping water, with battle axes drawn, Adelma had never felt more alive.

"What the—"

The sentries both jumped to their feet, knocking their stools over.

Adelma leapt at them, and in two swift moves sent the flat sides of her axes crashing into both their heads. One collapsed, but the other obviously had a harder skull, or she hadn't hit him as hard. He merely staggered then let out a shout of alarm.

She dropped to a crouch and swiped the back of her axe at the back of his knees, knocking him to the deck. She hit him again, this time harder, and then she smashed the alchemical globe.

She heard the third sentry below moving, probably grabbing a weapon. She got ready at the trapdoor, waiting for him to surface.

This was what she was made for. The exhilaration of the fight coursed through her body. She felt strong and powerful. Limitless. Assurak thought he could mess with her? Well, he had another thing coming.

Hit them back stronger and faster than they'd expect.

He'd expect her to be floored by the loss of her boat. She'd show him.

Although, she would have to be quick about it—the sentry's shout could very well have been heard. In which case, she would have very little time to get away before Assurak's remaining ship came after her.

***

Her attack on the three sentries finished, Adelma was about to drag the unconscious men off the ship when she heard the thump of someone stepping aboard. She whirled, drawing her axes. The man was big—huge.

"Radish," she whispered, dismayed. He carried the bundle of her clothes, her potion, and the opium container.

"Adelma, the hell you doing?" he whispered back. "This is a damned stupid idea. A really bad idea."

"What the hell are *you* doing here?"

"Mercy told me about your plan so I could come help you."

Adelma groaned inwardly. "Bloody Mercy." She heaved one of the sentries towards the gang plank. "That's mighty nice of her, but I don't need help."

"You're taking the opium to Teraverre, ain't you?"

"Not your business. Put my stuff down and leave." Adelma threw the first sentry onto the docks. "D'you hear me? I said get out of here."

Radish shook his head. "I'm not letting you do this. Assurak will give chase. He'll never let it go. And he won't do it alone, either. D'you even know how to work a steam engine?"

Adelma threw the second sentry onto the docks. The unconscious man fell heavily onto the flagstones—that would hurt come morning. She went to grab the final one. "I know the basics." Mercy had explained the theory of it. *Besides, how hard could it be?*

"Seriously, Adelma. Stop this now."

Adelma threw the final sentry off the ship, just in time to hear the sounds of footsteps and shouting in the distance. Someone had heard the sentry and gone to raise the alarm.

No point panicking at this point. She was ready. Still naked, Adelma calmly untethered the ship.

"For crying out loud, Adelma, don't do this," Radish whispered.

"Too late."

"You can't navigate this ship alone, and Assurak isn't just going to send his ships after you!" Radish said, exasperated. "He has other contacts, too."

"Get off my ship."

"No."

"I said get off my ship *now*. And be quick about it, or there won't be enough time for me to get away."

"Then I guess I'm coming with you."

Adelma froze. That, she hadn't planned for. But she didn't have the luxury of time. More shouts rang out as footsteps echoed against the dock flagstones.

So she pushed the boat off and hurried to coil in the line controlling the main sail, catching the night wind.

"You're the most impossible woman, Adelma," Radish said. He put down Adelma's bundle and headed below decks. He paused at the trapdoor. "Impossible, infuriating, and exasperating."

There was the tiniest hint of a smile tugging at the corner of his lips. Adelma didn't have the time to focus on that, though.

The ship sliced through the water, away from the docks. She glanced back at the docks. People ran to Assurak's ships, climbing on board. She nodded grimly to herself and turned the wheel a fraction. The sail snapped taught, and the ship gathered speed. Below decks, Radish got to work on the engine, and it began clanking and wheezing, giving the ship a further burst of speed.

Even though Assurak still had a functioning ship, Adelma hoped that she'd bought them enough of a head start to get away.

CHAPTER 20

Dawn cracked an eyelid, the sun a thin red line on the horizon. Adelma's plan seemed to have worked, buying them enough time to get away from Damsport. But Assurak's crew was obviously very well trained. The ship she hadn't been able to disable had set off after them, so while they were ahead, they couldn't afford to slack.

"If not for that bloody jelly," Adelma muttered, watching through her binoculars as the ship gave chase. The jellyfish had left a red trail of burns on her skin where it had touched her. Adelma cursed it a couple more times for good measure.

She and Radish had a decent head start, and just one ship was chasing them. Unless she'd drastically miscalculated, *The Bream* should be faster, with both sail and engine working hard.

Adelma had thrown on her clothes, while Radish had yet to emerge from the engine room. Whatever he was doing, it was working. There was no way Adelma would have been able to do this on her own, she realised. She would have been far too slow to figure out the engine, and if she'd only used the sails, Assurak would have caught up with her by now. Much as it made her skin itch to have Radish with her, she was incredibly lucky he'd shown up.

Adelma lowered her binoculars and rubbed a hand against the shaved side of her head. She wanted to go check on supplies and see what cargo there was below deck, but that would mean seeing Radish. She wasn't sure what to say to him. Or rather, she knew she should thank him, but the thought of doing that had the words sticking in her throat.

Everything he'd said about arranging to kiss the woman on purpose ran through her mind, as did Mercy's assessment—weird though it was. It had never occurred to Adelma that she might have hurt Radish's feelings, and that was something else that made her feel all weird.

Apologising for it, though, was out of the question. For now, anyway. But all this hung around her, awkward and heavy, so she hovered at the helm, not wanting to let go and head below deck.

She sighed. This was ridiculous. She wasn't about to turn into a coward. She checked the sails over quickly and headed below. The door to the engine room was open, letting out an awfully loud clanging. Radish had stripped to the waist, and his dark brown skin was covered in soot that stuck to the sweat drenching his torso.

He was facing away from her, so it wasn't cowardice that made her slink past him and into the main hold. It was just coincidence that they didn't get to make eye contact.

The vial with the alchemist's concoction was safely wrapped in fabric and packed away, so even if the ship lurched, it couldn't fall and break. The opium container had been secured in place, as well.

The supplies were generous—there would easily be enough for a trip to Teraverre and back. And there was a bit of cargo—*The Bream* had been due to get the full cargo delivery the following day. A few barrels of salted pork, bags of spices and other dried goods that smelt like herbs, and a couple of boxes of fragrant tree barks. Adelma wondered if this was genuine cargo or decoy.

Either way, it would serve them well—there was enough here to justify a trip.

She returned above deck, quickly checking on the engine room as she passed. Radish was out of sight, probably poking about somewhere in there. She almost jumped when she reached the top of the ladder and saw him up on deck, at the helm.

"Engine will tick over for a while on its own now," he said. "Figure you and I should talk."

Adelma frowned and crossed her arms.

"I'm assuming we're racing towards Teraverre and that this precious container of yours holds opium?" Radish asked.

"Could be."

"I need to know what's going on if I'm going to be involved in this."

"I didn't *want* you involved."

"That's as may be, but now I am. And if it weren't for me, they would have caught you by now." He gestured towards the pursuing ship. "Sails ain't enough against a steam engine."

Adelma blew out air, releasing her arms. She wasn't going to be churlish enough not to recognise that. "You're right on that count." She hesitated, wrinkled her nose, and scratched her head. "Thanks, by the way." It occurred to her that her debts to Radish were starting to accumulate. He'd pulled her out of her burning ship, taken care of her burns, and given her a place to sleep. Now he'd helped her get away. That was quite the long list.

That would need to be evened out—her old man never let an unbalanced score lie, even if it was to his benefit. He'd paid back kindnesses as thoroughly as he did slights.

Radish raised an eyebrow. "Wow—thanks from the world's most stubborn woman. I must have done something right."

Adelma frowned, but before she could figure how to answer, Radish continued talking. "So what have you planned for the opium? How on earth are you going to get it past customs?"

"I ain't telling you my plans," Adelma scoffed incredulously. "After the stunt you pulled? Talk about showing yourself as unreliable."

Radish smiled, which seemed like a completely wrong reaction. "Let's talk about that."

"Let's not."

"Well, I wanna talk about it, so I'm gonna. And since you're stuck on a ship with me, you're gonna have to listen." Radish smiled. "Before leaving, you basically sent me packing," Radish continued. "You think you got the right to talk to people like you don't care if you throw them away, and then expect loyalty from them?"

Adelma shifted uncomfortably. She hadn't thought of it that way. She hadn't meant to throw Radish away. It had just been all… overwhelming, and she'd reacted in the moment.

"It's like I told you before, Adelma. I ain't gonna apologise for what I did. It might not have been the smartest move, but I needed to know. I needed to break through all your walls and see what was below, even if just for a moment. That seemed like the quickest way to do it, and it worked. You got upset. You got jealous. If you didn't give a shit about me, you wouldn't have cared. So now I know that all your posturing is just that— posturing." Radish grinned. "Like it or not, Adelma, I matter to you."

Adelma wanted to protest, to tell him that she didn't care, that he could go to hell, that kind of thing. What he was saying was utter nonsense, total rubbish, complete garbage. But all of those words stuck in her throat.

"That's fine. You don't have to answer," Radish said. "And look, I'm patient and tolerant. I told you I enjoy a challenge, and I meant it. Just don't mistake me for a doormat, because I certainly ain't one." There was a quiet strength to the words, and Adelma knew then that beneath Radish's calm, relaxed exterior, he was made of harder steel than she was.

"And here's one line you don't get to cross: we ain't sailing into Teraverre unless I know what the plan is. The risks involved are far too great, and I ain't prepared to take them blindly. If you don't wanna tell me, that's fine. You can choose between Assurak catching you up or dropping me off at the nearest port."

Radish's demeanour hadn't changed—his face was still open and his body relaxed, even though he'd basically just threatened her with an ultimatum.

Adelma scowled. She didn't appreciate threats or ultimatums. And yet she could see where he was coming from—sailing into Teraverre with a container of opium was a dangerous, *dangerous* thing to attempt.

You can only rely on yourself, my girl, her Da's voice said in her head. *And on me. But the rest—people will let you down. Never forget that. Always expect the worst and be ready for it. Then you hit back. You hit back harder and faster than they expect.*

Adelma examined Radish. He had hurt her, and hurt her bad. He'd had that power over her and made use of it, and she hadn't paid him back. Her Da would have had something to say about that. But even just the thought made her feel tired, made her limbs feel heavy.

Radish looked good, sweat carving tracks through the soot and grime that covered his bare chest. He'd stashed his shirt away somewhere. He looked strong, at home on the ship.

What would it be like to let all of it go? To enjoy being on the ship with him, in their mad dash to get away from Assurak? He was a good man—smart, tough, and straightforward. A good smuggler, too, from his reputation.

Adelma remembered the idea she'd briefly had of the two of them partnering up, using her boat and his connections. If she'd gone ahead with that, her Da's boat wouldn't have burnt. Regret pinched her stomach. But regret was pointless. Things were what they were, and that was that.

Always retaliate, my girl. Always. Harder and faster than they expect.

The reason she hadn't partnered up with Radish was because of what *he'd* done. If she let that slide, what did that mean? That she was growing soft and gradually letting people like Assurak get away with things?

Then again, Mercy had a kind of an unlimited credit line—Adelma would never retaliate against anything Mercy did, ever. Not matter how bad it was. Could it be like that with other people?

With how many other people? How far do you go before you become a doormat?

Adelma pushed the heels of her hands against her eyes. It was all growing so confused. There was no way she could have let Assurak get away with what he did. That had been clear at the time, but now her Da's boat had burnt, and she'd lost everything she owned, including her house. Were things better now than the day she'd met Assurak? What had retaliating really brought her? Adelma didn't really know anymore.

"I'd make your mind up fast," Radish said, not unkindly.

She opened her eyes to find him looking back at Assurak's ship with binoculars. "What's going on?"

"Assurak obviously took the time to send words to some of his contacts." Radish handed Adelma the binoculars.

Her stomach sank. Two new ships now sailed either side of Assurak's. Their engines belched out thick pillars of smoke.

"*Flying Jack*'s portside. *Dead Rose* starboard," Radish said. "You know them?"

He nodded. "Pirates. If we're gonna get away from them, we can't be hesitating. We need to be all in. So I need to know the deal, or I ain't playing."

Adelma took a deep breath. He was right—this was no time for second-guesses. Her stomach jolted, and she once again got that horrid feeling that she was standing on the edge of something and that she was going to fall, fall, fall…

She took a second, ragged breath.

"Fine." She licked her lips. "Fine." But the words wouldn't come. She cleared her throat. "You ain't got no one but me to talk to between now and Teraverre anyway, so you can't tell no one. You can't betray me."

"That's very true, not that I would anyway." He waited.

Adelma cleared her throat again. "And once the drop's been made, my deal with the Widow will stand. Even if you go telling people about my plans."

"I won't do that, but yes, that's also true about your deal with the Widow."

"Alright then." Adelma glanced back at the pursuing ships. *Dammit, why is it so hard?*

Everything in her body was pulling back, alarm bells in her mind warning her that she was about to do something incredibly dangerous.

"Well, it's like this." Getting the words out felt like pushing a boulder up a muddy hill. "I got something, um…" *Dammit, woman, spit it out and get it over and done with.* "I got something what will make me look sick as a dog."

There. It was out.

"Like proper bad," she continued. "When we arrive in Teraverre, we have both the distress and disease flags hoisted. We go to the priority channel where there ain't no dogs. I checked, and Mercy confirmed. They let us through to the quarantine dock."

Adelma had never felt more vulnerable, more exposed. "And that's all you need to know," she wheezed, some odd pressure squeezing her lungs. She couldn't tell him the rest. It wasn't physically possible. The opium container was an adaptation of her Da's lobster pots. She *couldn't* tell anyone else that secret.

Radish frowned. "And what happens after the quarantine dock? How d'we get the dream to shore?"

"I've got something setup so the opium will get collected from the quarantine dock after we leave."

No more. Nothing more.

Radish cocked his head, eyes narrowed. "Stone the gulls, you're a hard nut to crack." He shook his head.

Something occurred to Adelma then. "You ain't asked me about how we split the payout from the Widow."

He looked at her in a way that made her feel funny. "I'm not in this for the money. We'll figure something out later."

Adelma looked away, bringing up the binoculars so she had something else to focus on. "Does that, um… does that mean that you're in?"

Radish took a deep breath. "Yes. I can make my peace with not knowing the full plan. For now."

Adelma felt weak with relief.

"And playing sick to use the quarantine dock is pretty elegant," Radish added. "Simple but effective."

Adelma felt a flush of pleasure at the praise from a seasoned smuggler, even though she already knew it was a good plan.

"It ain't replicable or scalable, though," he pointed out.

"This is a one time deal to impress the Widow into hiring me. It doesn't need to be."

"Fair enough." Radish grinned slowly. "Reckon it'll be fun to hand Assurak's arse to him on a plate. Always wanted to bring him down a peg or two."

Adelma felt herself smiling in response.

CHAPTER

21

Adelma helmed while Radish watched their pursuers through the binoculars. The two new ships were fast—much faster than Assurak's ship.

"*The Jack* and *The Rose* are fast and aggressive—built for the hunt. We can't outrun them, not over a long distance. *The Bream*'s designed to be fast and nimble, but discrete. Those two don't care about subtlety—we can't compete with that."

Adelma glanced back. Both ships had powerful engines that sent out towers of black smoke to the sky. "Their engines are clearly bigger than ours."

"Exactly."

They swapped places so Adelma could take the binoculars for a time.

The Rose didn't have any sails, which looked wrong, like a person missing their legs. Adelma guessed it had been built specifically to use a steam engine, whereas ships like *The Bream* were sail ships that had been converted to have an engine, as well.

The Rose also had odd vertical poles along both sides. *Something to do with the engine?* Adelma hadn't seen that before. *The Flying Jack* looked more like a regular ship. Its white sails billowed out, and it moved sleek and graceful—a far cry from its sail-less neighbour.

Adelma lowered the binoculars. "So we get ready for a fight. What are them long poles on *The Rose?*"

Radish shook his head. "No idea. I ain't had much dealings with them. Nothing against pirates in general—good profession, that—but them two are nasty crews."

"You got weapons?"

"My cutlass and a dagger." Radish pulled them out. They were practical blades, the kind that had seen many years and much action, but they also showed the care their owner took in maintaining them. Edges sharp enough to shave with—just the kind of weapons you'd want to get this kind of work done. "We should get ready."

Getting ready involved throwing overboard any heavy, nonessential items, including the barrels of salted pork. *The Bream* needed to be as light as possible to be as fast and nimble as she could.

Radish did some more tinkering with the engine and insisted on showing Adelma the essentials in case she had to operate it alone. It all seemed ridiculously complicated—much more so than sails and wind. And boring, too. Adelma decided there and then that she didn't like steam engines. Only one thing really stuck in her mind—the pressure valve.

"Basically, if it gets damaged or blocked, the engine blows," Adelma said, summarising Radish's detailed explanation.

"Pretty much. There's a way I can use it to give us a burst of speed, but it's a one-off, and it won't last long. After that, we can't use it again without risking the engine blowing. So it's gotta be at just the right time."

Back up on deck, Adelma examined the pursuing ships again. Assurak's original ship was trailing far behind. It was fast, but nothing to match the brute strength of the other two. *The Dead Rose* to starboard had brought its long poles down across its deck, and there was clearly some activity around them, although Adelma couldn't figure out what they were doing. One thing was clear, though—they were getting uncomfortably close.

***

The Flying Jack caught up to them first. Adelma hadn't dealt with pirates before—fishing boats didn't make interesting targets. As far as she could tell, pirates looked no different from the cut-throats and thieves of the Rookery—just that they were at sea rather than in a narrow alleyway. They were laughing and joking amongst themselves. Clearly, they weren't expecting much of a struggle since Adelma and Radish were only two. Well, they would soon find out the error of their assumptions.

Some of the pirates at the bow were busy with something, but they were blocking Adelma's view. She turned back to speak to Radish.

"Brace for impact!" he shouted.

Something smashed into *The Bream*'s stern in a sickening crunch of broken wood. It hit with such force that Adelma staggered and almost fell. The hull groaned in protest, creaking disturbingly.

The pirates at the bow had been setting up some kind of huge harpoon, and it had shot a massive bolt tied to a chain into *The Bream*'s stern. The chain snapped taught, stopping the little ship from moving away.

"We hack it out," Adelma growled. "Never mind the damage to the hull."

"*The Rose* is going to board us," Radish warned.

And indeed it was drawing up level with them.

Adelma grinned and drew her battle-axes. "Let them come."

Radish secured the helm so *The Bream* would stay its course, then he grabbed her chin and quickly kissed her. "Don't do anything stupid, and we might make it out of this alive. We need to hold out for a time—I have a plan…"

Before he could say anything more, the boarding began.

The tall poles on *The Rose* were released, a counterweight at their base making them swing. Two of the three poles swung towards *The Bream*, each pole carrying two pirates.

"I'll take the bow; you take the stern," Radish told her calmly as if they were facing nothing more than a minor inconvenience. He moved away, unhurried.

The pirates released their hold on the top of the poles and jumped, landing on *The Bream*'s deck. Adelma felt a brief flash of nerves. She was a good fighter—as evidenced by her many victories at the Old Girl's Arms—but she'd never been in a fight where the stakes were so high.

And then there was no chance to think about anything. One of the pirates had a long lance-like weapon with mean spikes beneath the main blade. He rushed towards Adelma while the second pirate, a woman, held back, slowly swinging a length of chain.

Adelma side-stepped away from the lance, deflecting it further with one of her axes. The man wielding it moved like water, flowing with his lance as if he'd expected Adelma to deflect. Maybe he had.

He twirled the lance around him as he spun away, and Adelma narrowly avoided it slicing her guts open. She deflected again and moved to attack, but he kept her at bay easily.

On *The Rose*, his crewmates cheered. They were watching the show, Adelma realised. The thought angered her, but no matter how she attacked, she couldn't get in range.

The thought of the other pirates had distracted her, and she parried too slowly. One of the spikes cut a mean slice into her left bicep. The pirates hooted and cheered.

Adelma roared her anger. She gave up trying to attack cleverly. "Don't do anything stupid," Radish had said. He'd probably meant that she shouldn't charge the pirate head-on, but Adelma was too angry to care. She had battle-axes, dammit.

She dodged past the blade of the lance, stepping past it, and allowed the handle to crack her painfully in the shoulder. She ignored the feeling, twisting and catching the lance handle under her left arm. Then she hacked down on it with all her might with her right axe.

The wood of the lance might have been hard, but it was still wood.

She flung the lance blade and its spikes into the water. The pirate tried to attack with the remains of the lance, but Adelma had unsettled him enough that his move was sloppy. She dodged easily and smashed her forehead into the bridge of his nose.

The man made a gurgling sound as his nose broke, staggering back. Adelma would have followed with a killer blow with her axes, but her head exploded with light.

She tottered.

Someone had hit her in the back of the head. Hit her hard. She swayed for a moment, trying to stop from falling on her face.

Things crashed back into focus as cold metal wound around her throat.

The woman who'd been holding back had wrapped her chain around Adelma's throat. It was so tight, she couldn't get so much as a finger in to release the pressure. Adelma dropped her axes, both hands grappling uselessly with the chain.

The pirate hissed behind her, "A gift from Assurak." If she'd been tall enough, the whisper would have been in Adelma's ear, but Adelma was a lot bigger than her.

So she threw herself backwards on the floor.

The woman made a vague sound as the full weight of Adelma's body crushed her to the floor, winding her, and the chain released. Adelma roared and flung the links away, pushing herself away to standing. The woman pushed herself up to all fours, but Adelma kicked her in the stomach and then in the face.

"And that's my gift to Assurak," Adelma replied. And then she picked up the woman and threw her overboard. "Tell Assurak that he's a piss stain in trousers what should learn to take care of his own business himself!" she yelled at the pirates still over on *The Rose*.

She turned back to face the remaining pirate.

Over by the bow, Radish had just finished dispatching his own attackers. "Adelma, watch out!"

Adelma had just enough time to grab her battle-axes once more before a second wave of attackers swung onto *The Bream*. This time, all three poles swung over, each carrying three pirates.

Radish came to her side. "Back to back," he told her. "And good fighting earlier."

"Pat me on the back later. When's your plan coming into action?"

"We're not there yet, but we're headed in the right direction. We need more time."

The pirates landed.

Radish fought well—calm and efficient, as usual. Not a single move that wasn't thought through or necessary. He used his cutlass for the heavy work, his dagger for quick killing stabs as he got in range of his attackers.

"What's the saying? Two's company, but three's a crowd?" Adelma called as she swung her axes. "What does that make nine?"

"It's eight now," Radish replied, dispatching one of his opponents.

Adelma ducked out of range of a mean cutlass and answered in kind with her axes. "Come on, you sponge-witted dock apes," she growled.

This felt like the completion of a lifetime of work—all the training her father had given her in how to fight, from that very first time as a kid with the knuckle dusters. Always retaliating, always fighting back—she felt invincible. Any nerves had disappeared, replaced instead by a sense of perfection that sang through her blood.

Her axes seemed to move of their own volition, blocking, hacking, and killing.

"We need to do something, or they'll just keep sending more until we tire out and can't hold them back," Radish called behind her.

She looked over at *The Rose*. He was right. They were getting ready to send another wave of attackers. Adelma and Radish were down to four attackers, but they couldn't maintain that pace forever.

Over at *The Rose*'s stern, Adelma could see the engine stack belching out its smoke.

"I've got an idea," Adelma told Radish. "Can you hold for a time without me?"

"Yes." Radish's face was grim with concentration, never taking his eyes off his opponents.

The Rose's pole at the stern began to swing, and Adelma raced over to intercept it. Instead of waiting for the pirates to land, she jumped up to catch hold of one. She swung her axe, chopping off most of an arm.

The man screamed and fell to the ground. He dragged his partner with him, and Adelma kicked them away. The pole began to swing back, lifting Adelma towards the sky with frightening speed.

She arced high over the sea, the movement and momentum making her stomach feel like it was being squeezed and pushed up into her chest.

Then the pole reached vertical, bringing Adelma high up above the edge of *The Rose*. The lack of sails made it look weirdly wide and flat beneath her. The pirates rushed about, a number of them clustering where the pole was going to land.

The counterweight at the base continued to swing, and the pole swung down towards the deck. Adelma didn't wait for it to reach the ground, though.

She braced her feet against it and then pushed away, releasing the handle and jumping sideways, towards the stern.

Her landing sent a painful jolt up her knees, even though she rolled to reduce impact. She heard yelling, but she didn't turn to face her attackers as they'd expected. Instead, she sprinted along the wide, uninterrupted surface of the deck towards the stern. The ship wasn't as cramped as a sailboat, giving her the room to dodge and weave.

A man charged her from the right, but she parried, retaliating with her left axe. The corner of the blade caught him in the shoulder and sent him reeling. Adelma didn't pause to finish him off.

Her whole body was focused on one thing and one thing alone: the pressure valve of the steam engine.

All of Radish's detailed instructions had fled from her mind with the pressure of the battle, except for one. Block the safety valve, and the engine blows.

She reached the engine stack—a wide chimney that spewed acrid black smoke. The back of the boiler stuck out from the ship's stern like an ugly boil. And there, like a barnacle on the boil, was the pressure valve. It let out a faint whistle and a continual column of steam.

Adelma raised her axe, but something crunched into her ribs. Luckily, she'd sensed the movement and shifted enough that although the blow hurt, it didn't break bone.

Something slashed at her face, cutting the skin on her cheekbone. She deflected the next blow, swung around it, and buried her axe into the man's upper chest.

Adelma didn't wait to face the others. She smashed the pressure valve with the flat of her axe.

Then she ran like hell.

"The valve! The engine was already at capacity—it's gonna blow!" someone shouted.

Adelma took advantage of the commotion this created. She put her axes away as she reached the pole and jumped just as it began its ascent.

The man who was already holding on gave her a vicious kick in the stomach then pushed her head away to make her let go. His sweaty palm pressed so hard into her face, it felt like her nose would break.

Adelma held on for dear life, struggling to breathe, struggling to get him off her face.

Then the engine blew in an angry screech of twisted metal.

The force of it ripped through her, and she let go, falling into the sea between the two ships.

The cold water closed over her head, filling her mouth and nose, before she kicked and broke the surface once more, gulping in air. Around her, bits of wood and metal fell to the water.

Adelma blinked, feeling the familiar sting of salt water in her eyes, momentarily disorientated. Then things came back into focus. *The Rose* had been brought to a standstill by its busted engine and partly destroyed stern.

The Bream, however, was still moving. Even with the harpoon stuck in its arse, keeping it tethered to *The Flying Jack*, it was still moving fast. Much faster than Adelma could swim.

She started swimming towards it anyway. "Radish!"

The Bream's stern was nearly level with her now. It was slipping away from her, cutting smoothly through the water. *No.*

"Radish!" she screamed.

CHAPTER 22

Adelma could hear the sound of fighting up on the deck—heavy blades hacking into something.

"Radish!" she screamed again, swimming as fast as she could, but her clothes, her boots, and her weapons slowed her down.

The Bream's stern passed her.

Adelma's heart was in her mouth. Would she be able to get onto *The Flying Jack*? Why would they bother letting her on? Better to leave her to drown.

Something wet hit her in the side of the head—a piece of sodden rope. Adelma grabbed it, trailing behind *The Bream*. She began to pull herself up.

Her arms burned from the effort, but she'd spent her life hauling heavy nets into a ship. She could work with that burn all day.

Finally, she heaved herself into *The Bream*. Using someone else's heavy cutlass, Radish was hacking at the wood around where the large harpoon had speared *The Bream*. Bodies littered the deck.

He glanced over at Adelma and grinned. "Impressive work with the engine."

"I try my best," she replied a little breathlessly as she dripped on the deck.

"So modest."

"I try my best at that, too."

She glanced over at *The Flying Jack*. Their relaxed, cheerful demeanour had gone, and some were bringing up containers Adelma didn't like the look of.

"I need you to helm for a moment," Radish told her. "And steer to port when I tell you."

"What? If we do that, we'll be broadside—"

With a groan of splinters, the last of the wood hacked away, and the harpoon shot back towards the remaining pirate ship.

"Bring us to broadside," Radish yelled.

"But—"

"Just do it!"

Adelma grabbed the helm and swung the ship around, presenting its side to their attacker. The pirates were too smart to give up such a tasty opportunity. A second harpoon connected to a chain hammered into *The Bream*'s port side. They fired two more harpoons—*The Bream* was well and truly caught.

"What now?" Adelma called.

Radish came to her side. " We're near to Traitor's Shallows."

"What's that?"

"No one knows. Maybe it was an island before or something—now it's a shoal of rocks very close to the surface in the middle of nowhere, with nothing above the water to indicate where they are. Traitorous for anyone what doesn't know it's there."

"Surely the pirates will know," Adelma said, frowning.

"Oh they will. But if we distract them…"

"Gotcha."

Radish took the helm. "We need them completely focused on us. When I tell you, we need to hack these harpoons out like I did the last one, fast as possible. Never mind if you make holes in the hull."

Adelma nodded, but before she could think of a plan to distract the pirates, something arced high overhead. It hit the mast and smashed. Fire licked out across the canvas sails.

"Well, seems they take care of their own distractions," she said.

"Over by the engine, behind me," Radish replied. "There's a hand-operated pump in case of fires."

Adelma got to work just as a second projectile hit the deck. The fire didn't spread across the deck as quickly as it had on the sails. She was working the pump as hard as she could, directing the hose and nuzzle up towards the flames. It was helping, but then a third projectile landed. She cursed.

"They obviously don't care about keeping Assurak's ship in one piece," Adelma called to Radish. "How long until we can move away? I ain't sure how long we can sustain this kind of 'distraction'!"

"I just need to get them into the right position…"

Adelma realised Radish was swinging *The Bream* around, but because it was tied to the pirate ship, it was slowly swinging both ships around. Very slowly.

Adelma cursed. She was focusing on the mast and the sails, but while she was getting that under control, the fires on the deck were slowly growing.

A deep clunk rang out, the wood of the hull groaning.

"What's that?" Adelma asked.

"They're pulling us in," Radish replied. "Dammit, we're moving too slowly. If we hack free now, we won't be at the right angle for the shallows."

And then Adelma saw a familiar iridescent ripple in the water just off to port, between *The Bream* and *The Flying Jack*. The perfect distraction, and it would stop them shooting fire.

"Hold on, I got an idea," she told Radish. "I need the net."

She dropped the pump and darted below deck. She found the net she was looking for. The weave was wide, made for carrying cargo rather than catching fish, but it would do. Black acid squid were large.

She hurried back above deck.

"D'you really think now's the time for fishing?" Radish asked. "Our ship's on fire, and we're going to be boarded any moment now. I think we're alright for fish."

"You ever felt black acid squid ink against your skin?" Adelma asked him, smoothly throwing the net into the water with movements that felt as familiar as breathing.

She could see the iridescent ripple of the squids within her net, but she didn't haul them up—not yet. She wouldn't be able to hold them for any length of time, so she would have to haul out the net and fling it onto *The Flying Jack* in one move.

Another projectile hit the mast. Flames sprung out merrily, rushing to consume what part of the sails the last projectiles hadn't hit. Adelma gritted her teeth.

She could see the pirates scowling over the rail of *The Jack*. The chains tied to the harpoons wound back in slowly, clinking as they did, bringing the two ships together.

Adelma could hear the roar of the fire and feel its heat, and she was itching to throw the squid, but if she missed, she wouldn't get another opportunity.

The ships drew closer still.

Adelma could make out the features of the pirates, could even see the missing front tooth on one of them.

She closed her eyes and took a deep breath. Then she grabbed hold of the net, her back and stomach muscles screaming to life as she heaved the net out of the water. The squid inside fluttered madly. She didn't pause, hauling it up overhead and flinging it onto the other ship's dock.

The net opened, scattering the squid all over the place. They squirted their acidic ink everywhere. They could squirt far, several yards, and screams rang out as the acid hit skin.

Adelma's hands and arms felt like she'd doused them in fire from the ink that had touched them, and she hurried to wipe it off with her shirt.

"Wash them off in the water barrel," Radish said.

"Water makes it worse." Adelma tore off her shirt and wiped off the ink as fast as she could, grimacing from the pain of contact with the acid burns.

"Here." Radish took off his shirt and threw it at her.

Over on *The Jack*, the pirates did exactly as Radish had suggested, dunking their burns with water. The screaming got worse.

"Give me one of your axes," Radish told her, appearing at Adelma's side. "We're right next to the shallows."

Adelma handed him her left axe.

He leaned over the railing, hacking at the hull where the harpoons were caught. He freed one of them, and the harpoon snapped back towards *The Jack*.

Adelma matched him, hacking a second hole in the hull, ignoring the burning across her hands. The moment Radish finished releasing the third harpoon, he threw the axe aside and ran below deck.

"Keep her straight while I put on a burst of speed," he yelled.

Adelma grabbed the helm and felt *The Bream* lurch forward as if it were a living thing. The engine made a deep guttural sound and then a disturbing whine as the ship shot forward like it had been spring-loaded.

The Jack continued forward, the crew still struggling with the squid. Adelma knew what it was like to have one of the buggers on board. Having half a school, well… that wasn't going to be pretty.

And then there was an awful crunching sound as *The Flying Jack* reached the Traitor's Shallows. The ship came to an abrupt halt.

Radish came back up above deck. He waved at a man standing at *The Jack*'s stern—no doubt the captain.

"Fair's fair, but I wouldn't want to be him," Radish said. "Worst feeling in the world, getting caught on the Shallows."

The Bream sailed on, quickly putting distance between them.

"How about that," Adelma said. "We evaded two pirate ships." She looked at Radish, feeling a grin tugging at her lips. "We made a pretty good team."

They exchanged a long look. Something fluttered in Adelma's stomach, making her eyelids blink a few times.

"I'd kiss you," Radish said, his voice a low, sexy rumble, "but our ship's still on fire."

CHAPTER

23

The fire had done some damage, but they'd gotten to it before things could get real ugly. The sails had been hit the worst. If not for the steam engine, *The Bream* would have a tough time making progress.

They set about salvaging what they could, gathering what remained of the canvas, and turning it into something usable. The mast was heavily charred, but luckily, it had been thick enough for the flames not to have time to get too deep. It would hold.

Adelma and Radish worked together, with Radish sitting next to the helm and using his foot against the lower half of the wheel to maintain course. He'd also helped bandage her hands using the remains of both their shirts—the parts that didn't already have acid squid ink on them. The bandages covered her palms and the backs of her hands, winding halfway up her forearms.

Adelma only had trousers and her linen and leather harness on—she had no change of clothes. But it was nice to feel the wind against her bare stomach and arms. And of course having to look at Radish without a shirt was no hardship.

Both of them had picked up a number of injuries in the fighting, but nothing life threatening. Adelma had helped stitch up a deep slice at his pectoral muscle, and they'd washed out each other's cuts. Radish also had an impressive shiner blooming on the left side of his face.

"I didn't see Assurak on either of those ships, did you?" Adelma asked as they worked.

Radish shook his head. "He must still be on the original ship that set off after us."

And that ship was a hell of a lot closer due to all the time lost fighting off the pirate ships.

"You reckon we can still outrun him?" Adelma asked.

Radish looked at the burnt sails with a frown. "It'll be a close thing if we do."

***

Every time Adelma checked, Assurak's ship was a little closer. He was catching up to them slowly, but surely—*The Bream*'s damaged sails were slowing them down. They couldn't afford to let up for so much as a moment. They raced towards Teraverre, as fast as *The Bream* would go. The euphoria of defeating the pirates wore off quickly.

They were both injured and tired, and Adelma's hands would make any more fighting difficult—her grip was weak. In short, they couldn't afford another confrontation.

If it came down to fighting, they might be able to survive, but Assurak would get *The Bream*. Then it was all over. Adelma truly would have lost everything. No deal with the Widow, no ship—she would be left without a pot to piss in.

There was no option but to make it to Teraverre first.

The Bream was holding it together, but the damage was showing. It was taking water through the holes left by the pirates' harpoons. The hull groaned, complaining loudly at the mistreatment it had suffered. Adelma talked to the ship in a soothing voice, doing her best to ease its aches and pains. She'd always felt that ships could hear when she talked to them, and she'd spent her whole life talking to her Da's boat. The reminder squeezed her heart and her throat.

She and Radish slept in shifts, alternating their time above and below deck. They'd fallen into a rhythm, working effortlessly with each other. It was like they knew what the other was thinking and could anticipate without needing to ask. It would have been enjoyable if Adelma weren't so damned tired.

What had been an exciting, daring escape now felt like a grim test of endurance. Adelma felt like her limbs were going to fall off. Her eyes were gritty with exhaustion, and her hands hurt like hell.

By the time Teraverre was finally in sight, both she and Radish were knackered.

"She's a good little ship, this one." He patted the helm. "She's done us proud."

Adelma nodded. "I were thinking of renaming her, when I first stole her. Now I think *The Bream*'s the right name for her."

Radish gave her a look. "Don't get too attached. It's Assurak's ship, and that man would crawl over coals to get something back that were stolen from him. And if he can't get it back, he'll destroy it. You won't keep it long, no matter what you do."

Adelma wanted to reply that Assurak could try—that she could handle all he could throw at her, but the truth was that right now, she felt too tired.

"We should be at the Teraverri checkpoint in a couple hours," Radish said.

"I best get ready."

She retrieved the vial from below decks and returned to sit against the mast.

"Who d'you get the potion from?" Radish asked. She gave the alchemist's name, and Radish nodded. "He knows his business, that man."

Adelma nodded. It occurred to her that she'd gotten precious little information about what exactly the potion would do to her. She raised her binoculars, and she could see Assurak looking straight at her. He was at the front of the ship, his usually slicked-back hair messed up by the wind. His eyes were dark and hungry.

Now wasn't the time to worry about the effects of the potion. The alchemist had said it would be bad, and that was good enough.

"In for a copper, in for a silver," she muttered.

She downed the contents of the bottle, and then she waited.

An hour later, she had yet to feel anything.

Teraverre was growing closer. The sun was lowering in the sky, tingeing the volcanic peak at the centre of the island with gold.

Had she forgotten something? Had the alchemist instructed her to take the potion a certain way? She wracked her brains, but she couldn't remember anything. Then again, there hadn't been much time for conversation, given how she'd been threatening him. Maybe, in hindsight, that had been a mistake.

Teraverre got closer and closer, and still, Adelma felt fine. She focused on her stomach, trying to detect any kind of sensation there. By the time the queue for the checkpoint was visible, Adelma became worried. All the more so because maybe Assurak had realised his quarry would escape him. His ship had put on a burst of speed and was closing in on them.

Adelma considered pretending to be sick—anything to stay one step ahead of the bastard. But she looked over at Radish. Could she do that? Put him at that kind of risk? He had come along for the ride, sure, but she'd told him she had a way to actually *be* ill. That she had a way to truly convince the customs officers.

Her Da's voice rose up, reminding her that he wasn't family. That she should only trust herself. Adelma frowned. She was starting to resent that voice coming up all the time. And if she couldn't convince the Teraverri agents that she was sick, she would be in as much trouble as Radish.

Sometimes that voice was damned stupid.

"How long did he say it would need to take effect?" Radish asked.

"He didn't, really." Adelma hesitated, unsure what to do. They couldn't hope to outrun Assurak if they didn't stop in Teraverre, but they couldn't enter Teraverre with opium in the hold.

Then she felt something stirring in her stomach. Like the start of nausea after eating something bad. "Wait, I think it's happening."

"You think? You better be damned sure before we commit ourselves to going to the checkpoint."

"I'm pretty sure—" The spasm that shuddered through her back wracked her with pain, and she threw up violently.

"Alright, I guess we're on!" Radish jumped into motion, hoisting both the distress and disease flags.

Adelma tried to comment, but another pain spasm wracked through her, and she curled around the pain, groaning.

"Good, good," Radish said distractedly as he sailed the ship towards the checkpoint. "The more noise, the better."

Adelma didn't need any more prompting. She groaned and grunted, as she did her best to breathe through the pain. Something felt like it was clawing through her insides. She managed to look up once or twice to see the checkpoint growing closer. Radish brought *The Bream* around, angling towards the priority lane.

This was it. Was she convincing enough? Would she look truly sick? What if it didn't work? What if they searched the ship anyway? Or worse, brought dogs?

They'd hidden the opium container in the remaining barrel of salted pork. Would that be enough to hide the smell if a dog did come on board?

All the work she'd put in, weeks of planning, all for this one moment. She had to be so convincing that they sent the ship straight through right away. She rolled around on the deck, groaning loudly with pain. She was barely exaggerating.

Radish slowed the ship down. "We need assistance," Adelma heard him shout. "My first mate's got something real bad. We need to use your quarantine dock."

"Stop right there," a customs officer called back.

Adelma did her best to heave again, but nothing more came. The pain was, however, just as intense. She rolled onto her back, pretending to be wracked with shivers. She contorted her face, keeping her eyes closed, praying it would work.

"She's sick," Radish said. "She needs help."

Adelma opened one eye to take the scene in, and the light hurt her eyes. She certainly felt terrible, but did she look convincing?

"What happened to your ship? You had a fire? And those holes in the hull?"

"Pirates," Radish replied. "We managed to fight them off. Just about."

"Stop them—they're thieves," Assurak called from a distance.

Adelma opened her eyes to find the customs officer frowning at Radish. "Thieves?"

"This is *my* ship," Assurak shouted.

"He's talking nonsense," Radish said easily. "An old business acquaintance feeling sore over a bad deal he made. Not your concern."

"Is that why you came through the priority lane?" the customs officer asked, eyes narrowed. "And is that why the ship is burnt?"

"No, we came here because my first mate is sick," Radish replied, voice growing tight. "We need access to the quarantine dock."

"You seem very eager to reach the quarantine dock."

"Yes, because my first mate needs help," Radish said, exasperated. Adelma continued her groaning and curling around her stomach.

Assurak's ship pulled up at the floating dock behind them. "Thank you for stopping them," he called. "If you'll just help me to arrest—"

"Assurak, you piss-brained mongrel, stop bothering everyone with your nonsense," Radish shouted. "A deal's a deal, so get over it."

"What? What deal? I demand—"

"I've had enough of this rubbish," the customs officer interrupted. "If either of you want to access Teraverre, you'll go through the regular checkpoint."

"But we want to use the quarantine dock," Radish pointed out, his patience obviously fraying.

"Why would you want that when I just gave you an option to reach the shore?" the customs agent asked suspiciously.

Adelma's stomach sank. Radish had made a mistake, and the damned alchemist hadn't given her something that looked bad externally. She just felt bloody awful, but it wasn't dramatic enough to convince.

Radish frowned. "You'd let us come to shore? With Adelma sick? Last time I came here, you forced me into quarantine because my sailor had a cold."

"I don't believe she's sick. I think she's putting on convincing show, that's all. So get out of the priority channel. Go back to the main checkpoint for a full search."

Adelma felt like someone had kicked her in the gut. Literally and metaphorically. It couldn't be over so quickly. Mercy's information had been very clear: in the case of serious disease, the priority channel could be used, and ships were sent straight to quarantine. Radish had even been forced to go there for nothing more than influenza, for crying out loud! What were the odds that they'd found the only non-paranoid Teraverri?

She pushed herself up to sitting. It sent another wave of pain wracking through her body, and she grunted with pain. "I need..." she croaked. Her voice sounded like sandpaper rubbed over rock. Then she threw up violently. Sharp needle-like stabbing pain spread all over her skin.

"Patrician be kind," someone shouted, "look at her skin."

Adelma could barely think through the pain, but she glanced down at her stomach in time to see an ugly red rash was spreading across it.

She collapsed back, her head smacking against the planks. Her body no longer seemed to be her own, spasming and jerking as if she were a puppet and someone were pulling all her strings. Something foul rose up her throat, spilling out of the corner of her mouth in a viscous stream.

"Get her away from here immediately," the customs officer shouted.

"Let me take her to the quarantine dock, *please*," Radish said. "You're bound by international law to offer assistance to ships in need."

Adelma's head was full of an awful dizziness, her thoughts whirling round and round, and then everything went abruptly black.

CHAPTER 24

Adelma came to, but she felt so weak, she couldn't even think. Her world seemed to have reduced to the pinpoint of pain that started in her stomach, slowly stabbing outwards through her body.

"You're awake." Radish came into her line of sight.

"Where…"

"We made it to the dock. That was quite some performance out there. For a moment, I really thought you was in a bad way."

Adelma managed a watery smile. "At least we made it," she wheezed.

"By the skin of our teeth. This was way too uncertain a plan, given the risk. It's…" Radish pressed his lips into a line, obviously struggling with himself.

"Thinking it ain't the time to lecture me?" Adelma asked.

"You're getting a lecture, alright. I'm just saving it for when we're back."

"Assurak?"

"He went through the normal checkpoint, and he's now docked. He's got eyes on us, though. We make any move, and he'll be watching. There's a whole squad of coastal guards also watching us, too. We do anything, and they'll know."

"Hmm." Adelma would simply drop the opium in the sea once darkness came. The main thing was that she'd made it to the quarantine dock.

It wasn't, however, feeling quite like the great victory it should have been.

"That's proper nasty stuff, what that alchemist gave you," Radish continued. "How long did he say it would last before it eased off?"

"He didn't…" Adelma closed her eyes again. Even though the sun was low in the sky, the light hurt, like shards of glass stabbing straight into her brain. "He didn't say."

She felt Radish come and sit next to her, but she kept her eyes closed.

"Here," he rumbled.

She felt two strong hands grab her at the armpits and lift her. Then her head was resting on something—Radish's thigh. He lifted her head a little, and she felt the edge of a cup against her lips. The water tasted like the best thing she'd ever had.

"You seem to be very trusting of this alchemist, given how little information you have about the potion he made for you," Radish said carefully.

"He didn't give instructions only because I didn't give him much chance." Adelma explained about her interaction with him, about how he'd ripped her off on her Da's pain-killer.

Radish swore loudly. "Stone the gulls, Adelma, that's a bloody stupid thing to do. What if he'd given you a dud? Or worse, something real bad, like poison? Threatening people really ain't the best way to get them to help you, you know."

Adelma wanted to explain about retaliation, but she felt too tired. And now, with the pain from the potion still wracking her body, her logic didn't make as much sense as it used to.

Radish cursed again. He sounded like he was about to speak and then stopped.

"Is that another lecture for when we're home?" Adelma asked.

"So many lectures. Sometimes I think you're the dumbest smart woman I know. You're certainly the most infuriating."

"I'll take that as a compliment." Adelma gave a weak smile.

They were silent for a moment.

"At least you're keeping water down now," Radish said eventually. "I got real worried when I couldn't even make you drink."

Adelma realised that her leather and linen harness was completely wet. From the smell, she'd obviously thrown up on herself quite a bit more, but she couldn't bring herself to care.

"Are you really sure this is worth it?" Radish asked gently. He gave her more water.

"Yes," she replied between two gulps.

"Why? I get the loss of your Da's boat. I really do. But the rest—it's just money. There's other ways of making money without killing yourself over it."

Adelma finished drinking. "I have to make it work with the Widow. This will make my name, secure my place in the world. It'll set me up as a smuggler." In spite of all her weakness, Adelma felt a hunger at the words.

"Has it ever occurred to you that life doesn't need to be this hard? I mean, most smugglers didn't start off by going into a direct confrontation with one of the most powerful smugglers in Damsport and aiming to be hired by the biggest smuggling ring operator."

"I have to retaliate," Adelma replied through gritted teeth. "Assurak insulted me, and he had to pay. He blocked me from finding work. He destroyed my Da's boat. And now this. He's gonna pay for all this. When I get my deal with the Widow, I'm gonna *destroy* him. She's giving me his smuggling routes, for starters."

"And then what? Assurak will come for you—that's what."

"Ha. I'll come for *him*. That ain't enough to even the score. By the time I'm done with him, he'll be completely ruined." The thought made her tired, not excited. But that was only because she was sick at the moment. Once she was better, she'd have all the energy she wanted, and then Assurak would see.

Radish snorted.

"What? You don't think I can handle myself?" Adelma asked.

"Well, so far in 'dealing' with Assurak, you lost your Da's boat, we had a pretty nasty fight with some pirates, and you've made yourself so sick, you're weaker than a baby. You really sure you wanna take this up another level?"

"I can *deal* with it."

"I'm sure you can. But no one's immortal. Your old man weren't, and you ain't, either." Radish ran his thumb down the side of her face. "I'd like it if you stayed alive."

Adelma would have swatted him away, but she was too weak and tired. And it wasn't exactly unpleasant.

"You want to try and drink by yourself?" Radish asked her. He handed her the cup.

Adelma reached for it, but somehow, her hand missed entirely. She tried again, but her hand and her eyes just weren't co-operating. Her vision was doing something weird, too—like everything was vibrating.

She grimaced and tried to reach for the cup again, and she felt Radish freeze.

"I'm gonna stick my finger in your mouth," he said.

"Whaaa—" Before Adelma could finish formulating the word, Radish had stuck his index finger in the corner of her mouth, catching her upper lip and pulling it up to reveal her gums. He swore loudly.

"Don't move so much as a muscle. We're getting out of here *right now*. There's a port city near here, where they'll let us in. I know a man what can find us some help." He gently moved her head so she was lying on the floor once more, and he stood up.

"What's going on—" Adelma tried to roll and shift to sitting, but her body wasn't cooperating very well. Radish's big hands pushed her back down again.

"I said not to move a muscle." He was shaking, and his face was dark with anger. "What the *hell* were you thinking, threatening that damned alchemist?" he yelled suddenly. "That ain't a potion to make you *look* sick he gave you—that's poison."

Adelma felt a jolt of fear. "What?" Her voice sounded weird, distorted, reverberating in her skull.

"I seen the same thing happen to one of my guys, when a jealous woman had him poisoned. Same symptoms as you—gums turning black and trouble with hand-eye coordination. The more you move, the more it spreads through your system. We're lucky that the alchemist included something to make you throw up—could be some of the poison made it back out."

All of Radish's words sounded wrong, the vowels distorted and impossibly long.

"I'll do the opium." Her voice warbled.

"Screw the opium!" Radish shouted. "Ain't you listening? We don't get you some antidote, you're gonna *die*, Adelma." He passed his hand over his head. "Of all the things, threatening an alchemist and then drinking what he gives you. You bloody pig-headed woman."

He headed to the engine.

"Let me just," Adelma began.

Radish seemed to materialise next to her and shoved her back down none too gently. "You try to move again, I'll knock you out," Radish threatened. "We're leaving right now."

"No, please. The opium. Or I did all this for nothing. Please," Adelma whispered. "My Da's boat, all it cost me… I can't lose, not now."

Radish glanced at shore then back to Adelma. He rubbed his hands over his face. "Fine. Five minutes. Tell me what to do."

"What? No, it's gotta be me."

Her big moment. Her victory, getting the opium into Teraverre. But it wasn't a victory, was it?

"You tell me all the instructions, or we're leaving without doing the dream drop," Radish said calmly. All his anger seemed to have evaporated, replaced with his usual cool calm. "And if you waste any more time, we're leaving before you make the decision. You're not dying over your stubbornness."

"I…" She knew she needed to let go and tell him, and yet she couldn't. Or rather she didn't know how. Everything in her fought against it. It felt unbearable, this weakness. She'd relied on herself her whole life, just like her old man had taught her. He would be devastated to see her so weakened now. Useless. Needing someone else to swoop in and take care of things.

But he's gone, a voice whispered in her mind.

"Oh gods alive, he's gone," she said aloud. A new wave of pain—hot, tight, and completely different from the rest—unfurled, as if a stopper had been removed from a bottle.

"Who's gone?" Radish asked.

But Adelma barely heard him. All of a sudden, the pressure on her chest was such that she couldn't breathe. Her father was gone, and he would never come back. It wasn't Adelma and her Da against the world anymore. It was just Adelma, all alone, and she'd messed it all up. She was dying on the deck of a stolen boat, about to fail at her very first proper smuggling job.

Her throat seemed to have closed up to little more than the size of a pea, the air whistling in and out.

"Look, just tell me what I need to do," Radish said gently. He held the opium container in his big hands. Adelma had no idea how he was moving without her seeing him, but then nothing much was making sense anymore.

Something broke inside her then. She let go and told him everything.

Adelma wasn't aware of much. Sometimes she would see Radish's face appear in her line of sight. Although she distantly knew it was him, his face was all wrong, like it was vibrating, the edges melting into the air around it. The sounds made no more sense now—like she was hearing it all from underwater.

In fact, nothing made sense anymore, nothing but the tightness in her chest and the pain in her belly that sometimes made her scream out, even though her screams didn't sound like screams. They sounded like… She had no words.

At one point, she opened her eyes to complete darkness—pitch black. She began sobbing, sure she'd died. The darkness stretched for days and weeks—years. She spent years in that black cocoon. Years in the dark, all alone. Her Da wasn't there, either.

She saw herself at seven, felt the pleasurable pain of a punch delivered with knuckle dusters as she dealt with Mercy's tormentors.

Then she was ten, shaving the sides of her head so she could continue to learn drinking like her old man.

She was twelve, listening intently and repeating her old man's words back to him—there was no one in the world she could rely on. No one but him.

But where was he now? Why had he left her alone in the cold and the dark? Something twisted in her guts, and she wailed.

The sea poured into her mouth—the vastness of the ocean, filling her up. There was no space left for air in the dark. It was all water.

And then Adelma could feel things touching her. Something touched her arm, but was it her arm? What was an arm anyway? Or a hand? Or even a body?

Nothing made sense anymore.

She laughed, and the whole sea poured back out of her mouth.

And then reality slammed back into her with the force of a hurricane. She realised that it wasn't dark, that she wasn't alone. Instead, she was on all fours on some kind of table, throwing up violently.

"That's it… That's it."

She recognised the voice, but she couldn't focus on it.

"Make her drink more. Same again. She's got to drink it all, and then we go through the process again. Her body needs to purge."

"Drink, Adelma. Come on… That's it."

Something was in her mouth, pouring foul, salty water into her throat. She tried to protest but had to swallow to keep herself from choking.

When it stopped, she looked around her, disorientated. Something stung her arm, and she swatted at it. It was a man armed with a needle.

"Careful, careful—alright, here it comes. The next purging cycle."

And then Adelma remembered how she'd thought the sea was pouring out of her mouth. Radish helped her forward, towards a bucket.

***

It continued for what felt like an eternity. Sometimes, Adelma knew where she was. Sometimes, it was dark, the sea filling her up and leaving her again.

Adelma lost track of time, swaying in and out of consciousness. By the time her vision and hearing were completely back to normal, she was beyond exhausted. She was lying in a bed—some stranger's bed—and Radish was sat next to her.

"Where are we?" she asked weakly.

"A friend's. You remember the alchemist before? He got the poison out of you. It weren't pretty, though. And it were a close thing."

Adelma nodded. "We in Damsport?"

Radish snorted. "If I'd tried to make it to Damsport, you'd have died on the deck. We're at the nearest port city to Teraverre."

"How long was I out?"

"It's been two weeks."

"What?" Adelma tried to sit up, but Radish kept her down gently.

"You need to rest. Be careful. You very nearly died, and your body ain't in the best of ways."

When Adelma looked down at her hands, she saw the bandages were gone. The burns had almost completely healed.

"Adelma, there's a couple of things we need to discuss. First thing is Assurak took *The Bream* back."

At that, she tried to sit up again, this time in anger, but all she managed was a clumsy sideways movement that made the world swing on its axis.

"Easy. Easy," Radish murmured, bringing her back to lie against the pillows.

"How did that happen?"

"Assurak? You were dying, Adelma—priorities. I didn't really care if he took back his ruin of a ship, much as she was a good little one. Stupid move on his part, too. Now he can't claim we stole it from him and get any reparations from us once we're back in Damsport."

Adelma closed her eyes. Assurak was lining up more and more debts that she needed to pay back. "That's two ships he took from me."

"Yeah, but he didn't attack us, so that's a piece of luck. I got a very solid connection here, high up, so he couldn't risk it. A good thing, because we weren't in any shape for a fight."

"Two ships. He's gonna pay for that and with interest." Adelma made a fist.

Radish cleared his throat. "About that. I sent a letter home to Mercy, so she'd know we were alright—she worries, does Mercy, and I didn't want her making up some new, crazy conspiracy to explain why we were gone for so long. I told her about the poisoning and about the alchemist, too. I just received an answer from her today."

He produced an envelope with a number of stamps of it signifying international post.

"What'd she say?"

Radish cleared his throat. "That if she'd known you were gonna use that alchemist, she'd never have let you. He were the only one left your Da could go to because he'd alienated all the others on account of all the grudges he held against everyone."

"Mercy said that?"

"Well, I added the bit about grudges. She said about alienating people. But truth be told, after we'd been seeing each other for a while, a few people warned me that if you were anything like your old man, I should stay clear of you. I like to make my own mind up about people, so I didn't pay it any mind. But you should know that all everyone had to say 'bout your Da was that he took offence at everything. I don't think he were very well liked."

Adelma opened and closed her mouth a few times. "No that's… He just didn't let people walk over him. That's all."

"I didn't wanna say nothing before," Radish said gently. "Ain't right to talk bad about the dead, especially to their relatives. But this is different. That alchemist you used, well by the end of your Da's life, he also disliked your old man. A lot. Mercy reckons he probably sold you watered-down pain-killer. And then, when you threatened him, I guess he saw an opportunity to be rid of you, as well.

Mercy then goes on about her latest conspiracy about *them*, which makes no sense, but I think she's right about the rest of it."

Adelma sagged in the bed.

"You alright?" Radish asked gently, putting his hand on top of hers.

Adelma did something that was neither a nod nor a shake of her head. The way Radish had spoken about her old man. That he took offence at everything. There hadn't been admiration in Radish's voice, and it didn't sound like other people had admired her Da, either.

Her Da had been right, though, about retaliating against the bullies. That was how Adelma had made them stop. Coming at them so hard and fast they'd never dared bother her again. Getting back at the alchemist, though—that had been a big mistake. Real stupid, in hindsight.

He took offence at everything. Radish's voice rang in her mind again, and when she looked back at him, she realised that he'd left her alone, which she was grateful for.

Adelma's memories couldn't have been wrong—she had so many memories of her father being there for her, caring and strong, when she was little. But other memories bubbled up, ones she didn't like to look at so much. Times when her father had blown situations completely out of proportion. When he'd created massive scenes at the pub over the way someone had simply looked at him or at Adelma. Had it been respect in people's eyes as they watched the fuss, or dislike?

Adelma knew that Radish's judgement was sound. She sagged further against her pillows.

CHAPTER

26

It took a month for Adelma and Radish to get back to Damsport. Radish worked to get the money they needed to pay for their passage back. Adelma was too weak to help, so she had to rage and bite her nails in frustration at being forced to stay in bed like some weakling milksop while Radish took care of her.

It was like being rescued over and over again. Unbearable.

Eventually, though, they made the journey back. It was a far, far cry from what Adelma had pictured back when she'd first made her plans to smuggle opium into Teraverre.

That was another thing—she had no idea if the opium delivery had been made. Adelma hoped Dina and Two Planks were alright and that nothing had happened to them. Nothing about the smuggling run felt victorious.

So the return to Damsport was very subdued. The sea helped, though. Adelma was feeling stronger by the hour, and being back on a ship helped lift some of her low, confused mood.

When they reached the Enclosed Docks, a well-dressed man was waiting for them by the gangplank. "The Widow would like to see you both immediately."

Adelma and Radish exchanged a look.

"You don't have to come," Adelma said. "I can face the music alone, if there is music to be faced. You'll get half of any payout I get, though."

Radish shook his head. "She'll know I were involved either way. If she's angry, I'll find out sooner or later. Might as well get it over and done with. If not, well… It's always nice to hear good news in person."

They headed off with the messenger. Once at the Widow's compound, they were taken straight to the audience chamber. The Widow was already there, waiting for them, and the stench of walking into that room hit Adelma like a wall of bricks. She almost forgot herself enough to allow her face to show her disgust. She caught herself just in time, hoping the Widow wouldn't have noticed the slip.

"I'd heard you were involved, Radish," the Widow said.

"You know me. I like to get stuck in to the exciting jobs."

"Hmmm." Her eyes were as unreadable as ever, hidden behind her dark-black optics, and she held a cigarette in her right hand, smoke coiling slowly up from it. "Didn't you make some big bold declaration saying that you wouldn't work for me because of your so-called precious independence?"

"That's still the case, Widow," Radish replied. "However, when there were an opportunity for me to partner up with the person I reckon's gonna be the next big thing on the Damsport smuggling scene, I'd have been a fool to turn it down."

The Widow made a rasping sound, somewhere between a snort, a cough, and maybe a laugh. She took a drag on her cigarette, the tip flaring briefly. She turned to Adelma. "I never thought you'd pull it off. I never thought you'd manage to get my opium into Teraverre."

Adelma's breath hitched. *Pulled it off? It worked?* She took a deep breath, closing her eyes for a moment. Finally, the sense of victory that had been missing all this time coursed through her. Validation and fierce joy welled up, and in that moment, it all felt worth it. All that she had lost, all the pain, the confusion—all worth it.

She had made it. She was now a real smuggler—possibly the best in Damsport, given that nobody else had figured out how to get opium into Teraverre until now.

She re-opened her eyes. "Actually, it was *my* opium," she said casually. "I bought it from you, remember?"

"Ha!" The Widow coughed again. "My contact, though."

"Indeed. And because of that, I'll only require half the money your contact will be paying you for the opium."

"Half?" The Widow wheezed. "You're having a laugh, girl."

"I'm deadly serious. That opium run cost me my ship, my house, my belongings, all my money. We agreed to you refunding me the setup costs, but it ended up being a lot more steep than expected. Then I got my partner to pay, too—" She put a hand on Radish's shoulder.

The Widow took a drag of her cigarette. "You get half if you tell me how you did it. I heard about your ship being caught up in quarantine. How d'you get the opium from there to shore without anyone seeing?"

Adelma gave a small smile. "Fine, I'll settle for forty-five percent of the profits. Push me any lower on the price, and I'll go offer my services elsewhere."

"Word will be circulating about that job, if it ain't already," Radish said. "Plenty of folk would want such a determined and inventive smuggler working for them."

The Widow ground her teeth. "Fine. Forty-five. But that's not how I pay smugglers on regular runs."

Adelma smiled. "We can negotiate my regular fees later. I'll also need the black mark against my name lifted."

The Widow waved a hand impatiently. "I heard you and Assurak continued with that damned vendetta of yours. Don't you have better things to do with your time?"

"The black mark against my name removed, with you officially giving me your approval," Adelma said.

"And you wanted me to give you Assurak's runs, didn't you?" the Widow asked.

Adelma paused at that and glanced at Radish. His face was impassive, betraying nothing. She hesitated. Her Da's voice rose up in her mind, urging her to agree, reminding her of all the wrongs Assurak had done against her. Radish might have looked impassive, but she could see a tightness around his eyes. He was waiting to see what she would do.

And she knew then, knew it in her bones, that she if pursued vengeance against Assurak, Radish wouldn't stick around. That thought was more unbearable than leaving an uneven score.

"I don't care about having Assurak's routes," she blurted before she could think too much or consider the enormity of what she was saying.

The Widow nodded. "Glad to hear you've got some sense knocked into you. I've got plenty of other routes that need good smugglers. And then there's the matter of the ship you stole."

"What ship?"

"*The Bream* was earmarked for another client who's now getting angry because he hasn't got his shipment yet."

Adelma shrugged. "Ain't my fault if Assurak can't take care of his own ships."

"Clearly, you can't keep your ship secure, either," the Widow replied.

"No, but I made the meet anyway, didn't I? Has Assurak?"

The Widow watched Adelma from behind her optics, taking a drag from her cigarette. "Anyone tell you you're an arrogant little shit?"

"It ain't arrogance when you can back it up with skill."

"Ha!" The Widow coughed, her lungs crackling like old paper. "Ha." She took another long drag on her cigarette. "I think you and I will get along just fine, after all."

***

The following morning, Adelma awoke to a blinding headache. Though it wasn't anything like the pain she'd experienced when poisoned. This was a pleasant, familiar headache. The headache that followed a very good night out on the town.

She and Radish hadn't been able to buy a single drink anywhere in the Rookery. Word had got out about their feats in Teraverre and against the pirates, and everyone wanted to congratulate them, buying them drink after drink.

Everyone had assumed the plan had been hatched by both of them, and Adelma hadn't contradicted anyone, although Radish had, clarifying that the plan had been all hers. He'd only helped with the execution.

The night had ended after sunrise, raucous, loud, and fun. It was different, being out with Radish. Everyone liked him and wanted to talk to him. Adelma realised how different it was to make people like you rather than to make them fear saying something bad about you. It was a lot more fun, and she'd enjoyed being the centre of attention.

She hadn't seen Assurak, but she didn't care. All that he'd done until now no longer mattered. She was officially working for the Widow, so he wouldn't be able to mess with her anymore, and she was free to just let the whole thing go and ignore him. She also decided to let things go with the alchemist. She would never go to him for anything again, but unless she killed him, threatening him further would bring nothing good.

Adelma was shocked how light it made her feel to let all that go. She wasn't turning into some kind of saint who would turn the other cheek, but she could clearly see the part she'd played in causing things to escalate, so she was willing to wipe the slate clean and start fresh.

And didn't that feel good.

Adelma stirred, and she felt Radish stir next to her. It was nice, being back in his place. The smell was familiar, now, as was the sight of the whitewashed walls, the dark beams, the bright light that splashed the room, and the items from the faraway places that she still wanted to hear more about.

"Morning." Radish yawned. He smiled at her, and she smiled back. "So, now that you're the belle of the smuggling world, what's next?"

"I'm getting me a ship." The thought made a spike of excitement rush through her. The Widow had come through, and Adelma was incredibly flush, even after splitting the payout with Radish. "*The Slippery Eel*, she'll be called. Although, maybe I'll just get a sail ship for now, rather than a steam one."

She might be flush, but buying a steam ship was more than she could afford, and she wasn't ready to sink back into debt.

A sail ship was fitting, too. She would nail a silver to the mast for favourable winds. A nod to her Da, to his superstitions, and to his dislike for steam. He might not have been perfect, but he was still her old man, and he'd been the biggest influence in getting her this life she now had. She just didn't need to follow his teachings *exactly*.

Also, much as steam was faster, Adelma liked sailing too much to rely on an engine. It felt lazy, and ships without sails just looked too ugly. It was fine for a person to look ugly, but not for a ship.

"Slippery Eel's a good name." Radish smiled. "And what about everything else?"

"Everything?"

"You know, where you're gonna live, and all that."

"Oh." She hadn't thought about that.

"I think you should move in with me," Radish said.

"Oh?"

"Yeah." He leaned across until he was whispering in her ear. "I reckon I might be falling in love with you."

Adelma started so violently that she rolled off the bed and crashed into the bedside table.

Epilogue

Two Planks followed his mother nervously. "What about if there's storms?" he asked, stopping for the third time in his tracks. "Sky looks pretty dark."

And he was right. Heavy, leaden clouds hung ominously in the sky.

"Storms, I can handle," Adelma told him. "I been sailing longer than you been holding a broom."

"I been holding a broom a *real* long time," Two Planks replied, frowning.

"So that tells you she's got lots of experience," Radish said.

"Hmm, that's true," Two Planks said hesitantly.

"It will be fine, love." Dina took his hand and patted it soothingly.

They reached the docks, and Adelma's eyes settled on her ship. *The Slippery Eel.* A beauty, it was. It needed a crew, really—it was a bit tight with just her and Radish, so next thing she would do would be to hire herself a good first mate.

This trip back to Teraverre was *The Eel's* maiden voyage, and Adelma was here to make good on her promise to Dina and Two Planks.

"What about if the wind knocks the boat over?" Two Planks asked, stopping once again.

"Well, if the wind gets too strong, we reef the sails," Radish explained gently. "Make them smaller, see, and the wind can't catch the sails too bad if they're all tiny. Your Ma told us you were tiny when you was little?"

"Yeah, like a thumb," Two Planks replied at once.

"The wind couldn't knock you over then, could it?"

"I guess not..." Two Planks took two more steps and stopped. "What about the waves?"

Adelma grinned. "We just ride 'em. And I'll tell you what else, Two Planks—riding them big storm waves is fun. The ride of your life."

Two Planks looked utterly unconvinced, but he began walking again, following behind his mother.

"Have you got a story you could tell him?" Dina murmured to Adelma. "He responds best to stories. I don't know enough about the sea and the storms, but is there a story you could tell him about it?"

Adelma thought for a time as they walked towards *The Slippery Eel.* Her ship.

"Two Planks," she called, "you ever heard about krakens?"

Two Planks frowned and shook his head.

"They're mighty big creatures. Bigger than us. The giants of the sea. In many ways, they're like us, see. People are scared of them on account of their size, but in fact, krakens are very smart creatures. And very gentle. Female krakens make very good mothers, too. They carry their babies in their tentacles, to keep them safe."

They reached the ship, and Adelma stepped across the gangplank. "It's mighty rare to see a kraken, because they're shy. Again, people make up stories about krakens attacking ships and all sorts—but that's just nonsense."

"What do they do, then?" Two Planks asked, crossing the gangplank easily, now that his attention was focused on something else.

"They like storms. They come out with the big waves and ride them, just like we do on our boat. And if you listen very carefully, when you're out at sea and there's thunder, you can hear them roar."

"Krakens roar?"

"Bigger and better than a lion," Adelma replied.

Radish and Dina joined them on the boat, and Dina gave Adelma a smile and an encouraging nod.

Adelma continued her story about krakens, making it up as she went along. She tended to the sails and checked the lines. She checked the supply of drinking water and food. All the while, Two Planks followed her, peppering her with questions.

"D'you think we might see a kraken today, then?" His previous fears seemed to have vanished.

Adelma grinned. "We very well might. If the storm breaks, you and your Ma will need to go down below decks. And then you should press your ear against the hull, see, and listen very carefully. Often with the waves and the thunder, it's hard to make out a kraken's roar. But it'll be there, alright."

"If I knock against the hull, will it knock back?" Two Planks asked excitedly.

"It might, if it likes the sound of you. Maybe it'll be able to tell that you're the same as it is—a giant among your kind."

Two Planks nodded enthusiastically. "Thick as two planks, they call me," he said happily. "I'm gonna go down below decks and get into position."

He lowered himself down the trapdoor.

"Thank you," Dina said to Adelma once he was out of earshot. "People sometimes get frustrated with my Slothum. I know he's a bit different, but he's not stupid. He just doesn't operate like us. He operates on stories." She smiled. "And that was a great idea about the kraken— he won't be frightened in the least if the storm breaks now."

Adelma nodded. "No problem." She smiled and slung an arm around Radish's waist as he came to stand next to her. "We giants are actually a pretty friendly bunch, no matter what people think."

Dina headed below deck while Adelma and Radish finished getting the ship ready to go.

Then *The Slippery Eel* slid off, sleek and graceful, her bow slicing through the water. Radish stood next to Adelma while she helmed.

Once they were out at sea, she let go of the wheel, turned to him, and kissed him. He wrapped his arms around her, holding her tight. His body felt hard and strong against hers. His mouth was warm and hungry, making her feel both happy and dizzy.

When they broke apart, she leaned her forehead against his jaw. The wind tugged at her plait, the waves slapping playfully against the ship's hull. The moment was beautiful in its perfection.

Her old man had had it complete

ly wrong. Adelma could rely on herself, but she could rely on Radish, too. He would be here for her, no matter what came—she knew it in her *bones*.

And didn't that make the world a better place.

The Adventure Continues...

Longinus is looking for a wife
The Varanguards have been suspended
Trouble is brewing in Damsport, and not just because Longinus is trying to
make avocado shirts the next hot fashion item...

Go to **celinejeanjean.com/veiledwar** to grab *The Veiled War* now.

PS: If you enjoyed the series so far, leaving a review will help other readers
discover the series. Even just one line makes a big difference !

Dear Reader,

I hope you've enjoyed your time in The Viper and the Urchin universe so far. If you want more, I've got lots of goodies for you!

In *The Assassins' Guild*, Rory and Longinus are hired by the head of the Guild of Assassins to investigate an attempt on her life.

If they fail to get to the bottom of this, the consequences will be…unpleasant.

Can they navigate complex guild politics, survive deadly assassins, *and* do it all without arguing?

Then in *The Pickpocket*, discover Rory's origin story.

Lastly, you can get three bonus scenes that accompany some of the later books in the series. Go to celinejeanjean.com/bonuses.